The Usborne Beginner's Cookbook

Fiona Watt

Designed by Mary Cartwright
Illustrated by Kim Lane
Photography by Howard Allman

Recipes by Roz Denny, Julia Kirby-Jones
and Catherine Atkinson
Food preparation by Ricky Turner and Lizzie Harris
Cover Illustration by Christyan Fox

Contents

Cooking for Beginners	2
Pasta and Pizza	49
Vegetarian Cooking	97
Cakes and Cookies	145

COOKING
FOR BEGINNERS

Before you begin

Before you begin to cook any of the recipes in this book, read through the hints and tips pages at the beginning of the section it is in.

Equipment

Always read through the recipe you are planning to make, before you start to cook. This will make sure that you are prepared for everything you are going to do.

Sharp knife

Serrated knife

Slotted spoon

Wooden spoon

Colander

Vegetable peeler

Sieve

Kitchen scissors

Brush

Fish slice

Garlic press

Measuring jug

Large mixing bowl

Grater

Chopping board

Oven gloves

Baking sheet

The oven

Always arrange the shelves in your oven before you turn it on. If you have a fan oven, read its instruction book and reduce the heat, or the cooking time, by the amount suggested.

Ingredients

Before you start to cook, make sure that you have all the ingredients in the list at the beginning of the recipe. Each list shows both grammes and ounces. Follow the recipe using either grammes or ounces, but don't mix them up.

Taking care

When you are using a saucepan or frying pan, always make sure that the handle is turned to the side of your cooker.

Take care that you don't touch anything hot. Wear oven gloves whenever you put dishes into, or take them out, of your oven.

Don't leave the kitchen while you're cooking on gas or electric rings. Always turn off your oven, rings or grill when you finish.

Measuring with a spoon

You will need to use a teaspoon or tablespoon to measure some ingredients. Measure the ingredient as a level spoonful, not heaped up above the edge of the spoon, unless you are told to.

Dessertspoon

Teaspoon

A tablespoon holds 15ml (½ fl oz) of liquid or 15g (½ oz) of something like sugar.

A level spoon

A heaped spoon

Cooking hints

These two pages explain some of the cooking words and skills which appear in the recipes in this book. Read through them before you start to cook.

Breaking an egg

Crack the shell by tapping an egg sharply on the rim of a cup or a bowl. Push your thumbs into the crack and pull the shell apart.

Sifting

1. You sift an ingredient to get rid of any lumps. Place your sieve over a large bowl and spoon in the correct amount.

2. Lift the sieve slightly and shake it from side to side. You may need to use a spoon to push the last bit through the sieve.

Adding salt and pepper

Try adding a pinch of salt and three or four 'twists' of a peppermill.

In some recipes you will find that it says to add some salt and pepper. The amount you add depends on your own taste.

Beating a mixture

Before you begin to beat a mixture, put a damp dishcloth under your bowl. This stops the bowl from slipping as you beat.

Briskly stir the ingredients together with a wooden spoon or whisk, until they make a smooth, creamy mixture.

Making stock

Crumble a stock cube into a measuring jug, then pour boiling water into the jug. Stir it with a spoon until the cube dissolves.

Peeling potatoes

Wash your potatoes in cold water, first.

Hold a potato in one hand, then scrape a vegetable peeler towards you again and again to remove all the skin.

Grating cheese

Cut a piece of cheese which weighs more than you need. Grate some, then weigh the grated cheese. Grate more if you need to.

A garlic bulb *A clove of garlic*

Some of the recipes in this book include garlic. A clove of garlic is one of the sections of a whole bulb.

Preparing garlic

1. To remove a clove of garlic from the bulb, squeeze and twist the bulb until you split the outer layers of skin.

2. Slice a small piece off the top and bottom of the clove, then peel off its skin. The garlic is now ready to crush.

Using a garlic press

1. Put a clove of garlic inside a garlic press, like this. Close the press and squeeze the handles together tightly.

2. Run the blade of a knife over the holes on the press, to scrape off any crushed garlic which is still sticking to it.

If you don't have a garlic press, put a clove of garlic under the back of a spoon. Push down firmly on the clove several times.

Chopping an onion

Put the flat side on your chopping board.

1. Put the onion onto a chopping board. Use a vegetable knife to cut off the top and the bottom. Be careful as you cut.

2. Run your knife around one side to slice the skin. Lift a piece of the skin at the cut, then peel the rest of it off the onion.

3. Hold the onion like this and cut it in half. Put the cut side onto the chopping board and chop each half as finely as you can.

Tomato and mozzarella salad

Serves 4

4 large ripe tomatoes
4 tablespoons of olive oil
salt and ground black pepper
300g (10oz) mozzarella cheese
8 large fresh basil leaves

Use a serrated knife.

Core

1. Cut the tomatoes in half and cut the core out of each one. Lay each half on its flat side and slice them as finely as you can.

2. Arrange the tomatoes on four plates. Trickle a tablespoon of oil over each one. Sprinkle on a little salt and some black pepper.

3. If your mozzarella is in a bag full of liquid, slit the bag and pour the liquid away. Cut the mozzarella into thin slices.

4. Lay the slices of mozzarella among the tomatoes. Tear the basil leaves into thin strips and sprinkle them on.

5. Cover the plates with plastic foodwrap and leave them in your fridge for about 30 minutes, then serve.

Summer salad

Serves 4

1 small crispy lettuce
half a cucumber
1 large carrot
3 spring onions
a tub of cress

For the dressing:
3 tablespoons of olive oil
1 tablespoon of white wine vinegar
1 teaspoon of clear honey
a pinch of dried mixed herbs
a pinch of salt and ground black pepper

1. Cut the end of the stalk off the lettuce. Pull the leaves off and tear them into bite-sized pieces. Put them into a large bowl.

2. Cut the cucumber in half lengthways. Scrape out the seeds with a teaspoon. Cut each half into thin slices.

3. Use a vegetable peeler to peel the carrot. Grate it by rubbing it down, again and again, on the biggest holes on a grater.

4. Add the cucumber and carrot to the lettuce. Cut the roots and tops off the spring onions. Slice them into 2cm (¾ in) pieces.

5. Add the onions to the lettuce. Use kitchen scissors to snip the cress from the tub. Add it to the bowl.

6. Put all the ingredients for the dressing into a jam jar. Screw on its lid and shake it well. Pour the dressing over the salad.

Leek and potato soup

Serves 4

250g (9oz) potatoes
2 medium leeks
25g (1oz) butter
1 tablespoon of cooking oil
1 vegetable stock cube
dried mixed herbs
300ml (½ pint) of milk
small handful of fresh parsley
salt and ground black pepper

1. Peel the potatoes with a vegetable peeler. Cut them into small chunks, then put them into a large saucepan.

2. Cut the roots and the dark green tops off the leeks. Slice through the outside layer and peel it off each leek.

Stir the vegetables occasionally.

3. Wash the leeks thoroughly under cold, running water. Make sure that there is no soil left in the layers.

4. Cut across the leeks so that you get 1cm (½in) slices. Put the slices into the pan and add the butter and oil.

5. Turn on the heat and slowly melt the butter. When it starts to sizzle, put a lid on the pan and turn the heat down low.

Stir until the stock cube dissolves.

6. Let the vegetables cook gently for ten minutes. Shake the pan occasionally to stop it from sticking, but don't lift the lid.

7. Meanwhile, boil a kettle of water. Put the stock cube into a measuring jug. Pour in 900ml (1½ pints) of boiling water and stir it.

8. When the vegetables are cooked, carefully pour in the stock. Add a pinch of mixed herbs, the milk and a little salt and pepper.

Chopping parsley

Stir it occasionally.

9. Turn up the heat and bring the mixture to the boil. Then, turn the heat down so that the mixture is bubbling gently.

10. Let the soup cook for 15 minutes, until the leeks and potatoes are soft. Ladle it into bowls and sprinkle it with chopped parsley.

Put the parsley into a mug. Use scissors to snip the parsley into fine pieces. It is easier than using a knife.

Cheesy beef burgers

Serves 4

500g (1lb 2oz) lean minced beef
2 tablespoons light soy sauce
1 teaspoon dried mixed herbs
ground black pepper
40g (1½oz) Cheddar cheese
sunflower oil

Make sure that your hands are clean.

1. Remove the grill pan and rack from your grill and put it to one side. Turn your grill on to its highest setting.

2. Put the mince into a bowl and break it up with a fork. Add the soy sauce, herbs and two 'twists' of black pepper (see page 4).

3. Mix the ingredients well and divide it in four. Squeeze each lump of mixture into a round, flat shape (see tip, right).

Press the cheese into the middle.

4. Cut the cheese into four cubes. Press a cube into each burger. Push the mixture over to cover the cheese.

You could serve your burgers with ovenbake chips and salad.

You could serve your burgers in brown or white buns with lettuce and slices of tomato. Add a little mayonnaise too, if you like.

Space the burgers out evenly on the grill rack.

5. Fold a paper towel several times and pour a little oil onto it. Wipe it across the rack of your grill pan.

6. Use a fish slice to lift the burgers onto the grill rack. Turn the heat down to medium and cook the burgers for seven minutes.

7. After seven minutes, turn the burgers over, by sliding a fish slice under each one and holding the top with a fork.

Tip: shaping burgers

8. Cook the burgers for seven minutes more. Check that they do not become too brown. Turn the heat down a little if they are.

9. Press a fork on a burger to test it. If you like medium-cooked burgers they will feel springy. Well-done ones feel firm.

Dip your hands in clean, cold water to stop the mixture from sticking to your hands when you shape it.

Creamy fish pie

Serves 4

500g (1lb 2oz) of boneless, skinless white
    fish fillet (e.g. cod, haddock or coley)
400ml (14fl oz) milk
salt and black pepper
750g (1lb 9oz) of potatoes

2 tomatoes
4 spring onions
2 tablespoons of soft butter or margarine
2 tablespoons of flour
100g (4oz) frozen peas, defrosted

Watch the pan in case the milk boils over.

1. Put the fish into a saucepan. Pour in the milk, along with a little salt and a couple of 'twists' of pepper.

2. Bring the milk to the boil, then turn the heat down low so that it is bubbling very gently. Cook it for five minutes.

3. Take the pan off the heat. Lift out the fish with a fish slice, but don't throw away the milk. Leave the fish to cool.

4. Meanwhile, peel the potatoes. Cut them into chunks. Put the chunks into a pan and cover them with cold water.

5. Add half a teaspoon of salt and bring the water to the boil. Turn down the heat so that it bubbles gently. Put a lid on the pan.

6. Cook the potatoes for 10-15 minutes until they are soft. While they are cooking, use a fork to break the fish into flakes.

Slice across the onions.

7. Cut the tomatoes into small chunks. Cut the roots and the green tops off the spring onions and slice the onions finely.

8. When the potatoes are cooked, drain them in a colander over a sink. Put the chunks back into the pan, but not on any heat.

9. Crush the potato by pressing a potato masher down, again and again, on the chunks. Do it until there are no lumps left.

Mix it with a wooden spoon.

10. Add two tablespoons of milk from the fish pan and a tablespoon of butter, to the potato. Mix it well.

Turn the heat down to let it bubble gently.

11. Mix the flour with a little milk. Stir it into the milk, with a tablespoon of butter. Boil it, then let it bubble gently for one minute.

12. Add the fish, onion, peas and tomatoes. Cook for two minutes. Pour the mixture into an ovenproof dish. Turn on your grill to medium.

Use a fork to make the top of the potato smooth.

13. Spoon the potato on top. Put the dish under the grill. Cook it until the potato becomes golden. Serve it immediately.

Crunchy cheese omelette

For one person

40g (1½oz) mature Cheddar or Gruyère cheese
6 stems of fresh chives or 3 sprigs of fresh parsley
2 tablespoons of mini croutons
2 large eggs
salt and ground black pepper
2 teaspoons of olive oil

Look for mini croutons in the soup or snack section of a supermarket.

1. For the filling, grate the cheese on the coarse side of the grater (see page 4). Put the grated cheese into a small bowl.

2. Use kitchen scissors to snip the chives or parsley into the bowl. If you are using parsley, don't chop the thick part of the stalk.

3. Use your fingers or a knife to break the croutons into pieces, about the size of peas. Add them to the bowl and mix well.

You could add sliced tomato and basil instead of the croutons.

Page 4 shows you how to break an egg.

4. Break the eggs into another bowl. Add a tablespoon of water and a little salt and pepper. Beat them well.

You could serve your omelette with some lettuce.

The egg will set a little on the bottom.

Hold the pan handle in one hand.

5. Heat a small non-stick frying pan over a medium heat for a minute without anything in it. Then, add the oil.

6. Heat the oil for a few seconds. Carefully tilt the pan so that the oil coats the base of it. Pour in the egg and let it cook a little.

7. Use a non-metal spatula to pull the egg away from the side of the pan. Tip the pan to let runny egg flow into the space.

8. Keep pulling the omelette away from the side of the pan until all the runny egg is cooked. The top should still look creamy.

9. Spoon the filling all over the top. Tilt the pan at an angle and use a spatula to fold over one half of the omelette.

10. Leave the filling to cook for a few seconds. Turn off the heat. Slide the omelette onto a plate and eat it immediately.

Stuffed pancakes

Serves 4, makes about 12 pancakes

125g (4oz) plain flour
a pinch of salt
1 egg
sunflower oil
300ml (½ pint) of milk

For the filling: 1 tablespoon of sunflower oil
400g (14oz) lean minced beef or turkey
340g (11oz) jar of tomato pasta sauce
150g (5oz) of soured cream
50g (2oz) Cheddar cheese, grated

1. Put a sieve over a large mixing bowl. Pour in the flour and the salt. Shake the sieve until all the flour has fallen through.

Put a dishcloth under the bowl to stop it from slipping.

2. Press a whisk into the middle of the flour to make a deep hollow. Break an egg into a cup, then pour it into the hollow. *Use a whisk.*

3. Add a tablespoon of oil and two tablespoons of milk. Beat the egg, oil and milk with some of the flour from around the hollow.

The mixture will make a smooth batter.

Brush the oil quickly over the bottom of the pan.

4. Add some more of the milk and beat it again. Continue to add some milk and beat it, until all the milk is mixed in.

5. Heat a small frying pan over a medium heat for about a minute. Don't put anything into the pan at this point.

6. Put two tablespoons of oil into a cup. Fold a paper towel in half and roll it up. Dip one end into the oil and brush it over the pan.

The batter should sizzle.

7. Put the batter next to your pan. Quickly add three tablespoons of batter. Swirl it all over the bottom by tipping the pan.

8. Put the pan flat on the heat and cook it until the batter turns pale and is lightly cooked. Small holes will also appear on top.

9. Loosen the edge of the pancake and slide a fish slice under it. Flip the pancake over and cook it for half a minute more.

Make a stack of pancakes under the tea towel.

10. Slide the pancake onto a plate then cover it with a clean tea towel. Repeat steps 6-11 until the batter is finished.

11. Heat a tablespoon of oil in a saucepan. Add the mince. Break it up with a wooden spoon and cook it until it is brown all over.

12. Stir the pasta sauce into the mince. Bring the pan to the boil then turn it down so that it bubbles gently. Cook for five minutes.

Fill each pancake in the same way.

The dish will be hot.

13. Lay a pancake on a plate. Spoon on two tablespoons of mixture. Fold one side over the mixture, then roll it up.

14. Lay the pancakes, join-side down in an ovenproof dish. Turn on your grill. Spoon on the cream and sprinkle cheese on top.

15. Put the dish under the grill. Leave it until the cheese starts to bubble and goes golden brown. Serve immediately.

Crusty bread 'pizzas'

Serves two

1 ciabatta bread,
or 1 thick French stick

For the topping; 1 onion
2 cloves of garlic
2 tablespoons of olive oil
400g (14oz) can of chopped tomatoes
half a teaspoon of dried mixed herbs
salt and ground black pepper
250g (9oz) of mozzarella cheese
2 tablespoons of grated Parmesan cheese

*Stir it once
or twice.*

1. Cut the top and bottom off the onion and peel it. Cut it in half and slice it. Peel the garlic cloves and crush them (see page 5).

2. Heat two tablespoons of oil in a frying pan. Gently cook the garlic and onion, for five minutes, or until they are soft.

3. Add the tomatoes, the herbs and some salt and pepper. Turn up the heat and bring the mixture to the boil.

You could put olives or slices of salami or ham on top of the cheese, before you cook them.

4. Turn the heat down to medium and let the topping cook for about ten minutes, or until most of the liquid has gone.

5. Take the pan off the heat. Leave it to cool for 10-15 minutes. Turn your oven on to 200°C, 400°F, Gas mark 6.

6. Put your bread onto a chopping board and carefully cut it in half lengthways. Put each half onto a large baking sheet.

7. Spread each piece of bread with the topping. Slice the mozzarella cheese as finely as you can and lay the slices on top.

8. Sprinkle the Parmesan cheese on top. Bake the 'pizzas' for about 15 minutes or until the cheese is bubbling.

9. Take the baking sheet out of the oven and let the bread cool for five minutes. Cut each half into pieces, to make it easier to eat.

Try one with cheese, pepperoni and olives.

Cheesy spinach flan

Serves 4

350g (12oz) shortcrust pastry, thawed
if frozen
200g (7oz) fresh spinach
1 onion
2 cloves of garlic
1 tablespoon of olive oil
100g (4 oz) grated Cheddar cheese

2 medium size eggs
200ml (7floz) single cream
or full-fat milk
salt and ground black pepper

a 20cm (8in) flan dish or tin

Heat your oven to 170°C,
325°F, Gas mark 3.

Make sure that your work surface is clean and dry.

1. Sprinkle a little flour on your work surface and onto a rolling pin. Shape the pastry into a smooth, round ball.

2. Roll the pastry, turn it in a quarter turn and roll it again. Keep on doing this until you get a circle about 25cm (10in) across.

3. Put your flan dish or tin onto a baking sheet. Roll the pastry over the rolling pin then unroll the pastry onto the dish.

If you don't have baking beans, use dried beans.

4. Gently press the pastry into the base and up the sides of the dish, without tearing it. Bring the pastry over the rim of the dish.

Press the water out of the spinach with the back of a spoon.

5. Prick the base of the flan a few times with a fork. Press a sheet of foil into the dish, then fill the base with baking beans.

6. Put the flan into the fridge for half an hour and turn on your oven. Wash the spinach and put the wet leaves into a large pan.

Wear oven gloves.

7. Cook the spinach for three minutes over a medium heat. It wilts as it cooks. Drain it, press out the water. Leave it to cool.

8. Slice the onion and crush the garlic (see page 5). Put the oil into a pan. Cook the onion and garlic for five minutes, until they are soft.

9. When the pastry has cooled, put it into the oven. Cook it for 15 minutes, then lift it out of the oven carefully.

10. Lift off the foil and the beans. Trim off the pastry around the rim. Put the flan, uncovered, in the oven for five more minutes.

11. Turn your oven to 160°C, 325°F, Gas mark 3. Spread the onion mixture over the flan. Cut up the spinach and add it too.

12. Sprinkle the cheese and a little salt and pepper on top of the spinach. Beat the eggs with the cream or milk, in a small bowl.

13. Pour the mixture over the filling. Put the flan into the oven for about 30 minutes or until the top has set and is golden.

Pan-fried meat or fish

Serves 4

2 tablespoons of olive oil
either: 4 x 100g (3½ oz) sirloin or rump steaks,
    or 4 skinless, boneless chicken breasts,
    or 4 x 100g (3½ oz) skinless, boneless salmon fillets
2 sprigs of fresh parsley
salt and black pepper

1. If you are using chicken breasts, make two cuts on top of each one with a sharp knife. Put four plates in a warm place.

2. Put a non-stick frying pan onto a ring and turn it on to a high heat. Leave it for a minute without anything in it.

3. Pour the oil into the pan and brush it over the bottom. Add the pieces of steak, chicken or salmon. They will sizzle a little.

4. If you are cooking steak, cook the pieces on one side for two minutes, or for three to four minutes if you like them well done.

If chicken is cooked, the juices are clear, not pink.

If you are using chicken, cook the pieces for five to six minutes on one side. Chicken should always be well-cooked.

It makes it tastier if you leave it to stand.

For salmon, cook the pieces for about three minutes on one side. The fillets should still be a little juicy and not dry.

5. When you have cooked the pieces on one side, turn the heat to medium. Turn them over and cook them for the same time again.

6. When the meat or fish is cooked, use a fish slice to lift it onto the warm plates. Leave them to stand for few minutes.

This piece of chicken was cooked on a griddle pan. The browned stripes are made by the ridges on the pan.

7. Chop the parsley (see page 9) and sprinkle a little onto each piece. Serve the meat or fish with potatoes and a salad.

Lamb kebabs in pitta pockets

Serves 4
2 large lamb leg steaks, about 175g (6 oz) each
1 clove of garlic
half a teaspoon of mild curry powder
1 tablespoon of oil
4 wooden kebab or satay sticks
2 little gem lettuces
quarter of a cucumber
2 tablespoons of natural yogurt
1 teaspoon of dried mint, or
1 tablespoon of fresh chopped mint
salt and ground black pepper
2 pitta breads

You can squeeze some lemon juice onto the lamb before you serve it.

1. If there is a small bone in the middle of the lamb steaks, cut it out. Cut the meat into cubes, with sides about 2cm (¾ in).

2. Peel and crush the garlic (see page 5). Put the garlic, curry powder, oil and a little salt and pepper into a bowl and mix well.

3. Add the meat into the bowl and stir it well. Cover the bowl with plastic foodwrap and leave it for half an hour.

Throw away the core of the lettuce.

4. Put the wooden sticks into a bowl of cold water and leave them to soak. This stops them from burning under the grill.

5. Shread the lettuce by cutting across it and put it in a bowl. If you are using fresh mint, chop the leaves finely.

6. Cut the cucumber in half, then slice it finely. Mix the lettuce, yogurt, mint and cucumber, with a little salt and pepper.

Put the same number of cubes on each stick.

7. Turn your grill on to medium. Dry the kebab sticks on a paper towel, then push the cubes of lamb onto them.

8. Put the kebabs onto the grill rack and push it under your grill. Cook the kebabs for five minutes, then turn them over.

9. Cook the kebabs for five minutes more. While they are cooking, cut the pitta bread in half across the middle, like this.

10. Put the kebabs on a plate. Put the pittas under the grill for two minutes but turn off the heat. This will warm them through.

11. Run the tip of a knife along the cut edge of each pitta to open it up. Fill each one with some of the lettuce mixture.

12. Hold a kebab stick at one end and use a fork to slide the lamb off. Put some lamb into each pitta and eat immediately.

Vegetable stir fry

Serves 4

1 carrot
1 red or yellow pepper
2 courgettes
100g (4oz) mangetout
4 spring onions
100g (4oz) baby sweetcorn
1 clove of garlic
100g (4oz) fresh beanshoots
2-3 tablespoons of vegetable oil

For the sauce:
1 teaspoon of cornflour
1 tablespoon of light soy sauce
2 tablespoons of water
2 tablespoons of oil
a pinch of sugar

It's easiest to slice a pepper from the inside.

Cut the pieces about 5cm (2in) long.

1. Peel the carrot with a vegetable peeler. Cut off the top and bottom, then slice it into circles, as finely as you can.

2. Cut the pepper in half. Cut out the stalk and scrape out the seeds and white bits inside. Cut it into thin slices.

3. Cut the ends off the courgettes. Cut them in half lengthways. Slice the halves into strips then cut them into shorter pieces.

4. Snip the ends off the mangetout using a pair of kitchen scissors. Then, cut each mangetout into smaller pieces, with a knife.

5. Cut the roots and the dark green ends off the spring onions. Peel the outer layer off them, then slice them diagonally.

6. Cut the ends off the sweetcorn, then cut them in half lengthways. Peel the clove of garlic and crush it (see page 5).

Stir quickly with a wooden spoon or spatula.

These vegetables were cooked in a special stir-fry pan, but you can use a large frying pan or a wok.

7. Put the cornflour into a cup and add a few drops of water. Mix it to make a paste. Stir in the rest of the sauce ingredients.

8. Heat two tablespoons of oil in a frying pan or wok. Add the carrot, pepper and courgette to the pan. Cook them for three minutes.

Stir the vegetables as they cook.

9. Add the sweetcorn, garlic and onions. Cook them for a minute. Add the mangetout and beanshoots. Cook the mixture for three minutes.

10. Stir the sauce in the cup then quickly pour it into the pan. Stir it to coat the vegetables and serve them immediately.

Pasta with fresh tomato sauce

Serves 4

For the sauce: 8 medium tomatoes
2 cloves of garlic
3 tablespoons of olive oil
half a teaspoon of caster sugar

375g (12oz) dried pasta shapes
1 tablespoon of olive oil
salt and ground black pepper
6 fresh basil leaves

To serve: 40g (1½ oz) of grated Parmesan cheese

Pasta shapes such as shells, twists or spirals are best for this recipe.

1. Boil a kettle of water. Pull any stalks off the tomatoes. Use the tip of a knife to cut a cross on the bottom of each tomato.

2. Put the tomatoes into a heat-proof bowl. Carefully pour the boiling water over the tomatoes so that they are covered.

Use a slotted spoon.

3. Leave the tomatoes for at least a minute. Fill another bowl with cold water, then spoon the tomatoes into it.

4. Lift the tomatoes out of the water. Use your fingers to peel off their skins, starting at the cuts you made.

5. Cut each tomato into quarters, then cut out the tough cores. Cut the fleshy part of each tomato into small pieces.

6. Peel the garlic and crush it (see page 5). Heat the oil in a large saucepan. Add the tomatoes, garlic and sugar and stir well.

7. Turn the heat to medium and cook the sauce for about five minutes. Stir it once or twice as it cooks.

8. While the sauce is cooking, fill a large pan with water and put it on to boil. Add a teaspoon of salt to the water.

9. When the water is boiling hard, add the pasta and stir it once or twice. Bring the pan back to the boil.

When you serve your pasta, sprinkle it with the grated Parmesan cheese.

Drain the pasta in a colander over a sink.

Add a little salt and pepper too.

10. Turn down the heat so the water is bubbling, but not too fiercely. Turn the heat under the sauce as low as it will go.

11. Cook the pasta for the time it says on its packet, then drain it. Rinse the pasta under cold water. Put it back into its pan.

12. Add a tablespoon of oil to the pasta and stir in the sauce. Rip the basil leaves into pieces and stir them in. Serve immediately.

Prawn and pepper pilaff

Serves 4

200g (7oz) peeled prawns
1 medium onion
1 clove of garlic
1 red or yellow pepper
2 tablespoons of oil
15g (½oz) butter
1 teaspoon of mild curry powder
200g (7oz) basmati rice
400ml (14floz) water
50g (2oz) creamed coconut
1 teaspoon of salt
100g (4oz) peas
freshly ground black pepper

1. If you are using frozen prawns, spread them out on a plate. Leave them for two hours to defrost, then drain them in a sieve.

2. Cut the ends off the onion, peel the onion and cut it in half. Slice each half finely then cut the slices into small pieces.

3. Peel the garlic clove and crush it (see page 5). Cut the red or yellow pepper in half. Cut out the seeds and the stalk.

Stir it occasionally.

4. Slice the pepper finely, then cut the slices into small pieces. Make them about the same size as the pieces of onion.

5. Heat the oil and butter gently in a large non-stick pan. Add the vegetables. Cook them on a medium heat for seven minutes.

6. Stir in the curry powder and add the rice. Cut the coconut into chunks and add it to the pan along with the water and salt.

Stir it once or twice.

7. Turn up the heat and bring the mixture to the boil. When it has boiled, turn the heat down so that it is bubbling gently.

8. Cover the pan and let it cook for ten minutes. Don't lift the lid while it is cooking as the steam in the pan cooks the rice.

Add a little black pepper too.

Stir it to separate the grains of rice.

9. Remove the lid carefully and stir in the prawns and peas. Put the lid on the pan again and cook it for two to three minutes.

10. Take the pan off the heat and leave it, with the lid on, for five minutes. Stir the mixture with a fork and serve immediately.

Beef goulash with tagliatelle

Serves 4

1 stock cube
1 onion
2 cloves of garlic
1 red or yellow pepper
500g (1lb 2oz) lean braising beef
2 tablespoons of sunflower oil or olive oil
1 teaspoon of dried mixed herbs
1 tablespoon of paprika

1 tablespoon of wine vinegar
400g (14oz) can of chopped tomatoes
200g (7oz) tagliatelle pasta
1 tablespoon of butter or soft margarine
150g (5oz) soured cream or crème fraîche
salt and ground black pepper

Heat your oven to 170°C, 325°F, Gas mark 3.

Stir the meat as it cooks.

1. Make 300ml (½ pint) of stock (see page 4). Cut the ends off the onion and peel off the skin. Cut it in half and slice it finely.

2. Peel and crush the garlic. Cut the pepper in half and remove the core and the seeds. Slice it finely. Turn on your oven.

3. Cut the meat into 1cm (½ in) chunks. Heat the oil in a frying pan over a medium heat. Add the meat and start to cook it.

Add a little salt and pepper too.

4. When the chunks of meat have browned all over, remove the meat with a slotted spoon and put it on a plate.

5. Put the onion, garlic and pepper into the pan. Stir them well and cook them for five minutes, until they are soft.

6. Sprinkle on the herbs and paprika. Put the meat back in the pan and stir it. Add the vinegar, tomatoes and the stock.

Wear oven gloves.

7. Bring the mixture to the boil, stirring it as it cooks. Once it has boiled, ladle it carefully into an oven-proof dish. Put a lid on the dish.

8. Put the dish into the oven for an hour. Take it out and stir it. Put the lid back and return it to the oven for half an hour.

9. About 20 minutes before the meat is ready, fill a large pan with water. Add a teaspoon of salt and bring the water to the boil.

10. Put the pasta into the water and bring back to the boil. Turn the heat down so that it isn't boiling too fiercely.

11. Cook the pasta for the time it says on its packet, then drain it in a colander. Spoon the butter onto the pasta and toss it.

12. Put the pasta onto four plates or bowls and put the meat onto top. Add some cream or crème fraîche on top.

Cooking pasta

This shows yellow egg tagliatelle, but you could use green spinach tagliatelle for this dish.

When you cook pasta, start measuring its cooking time from when the water boils again after adding the pasta.

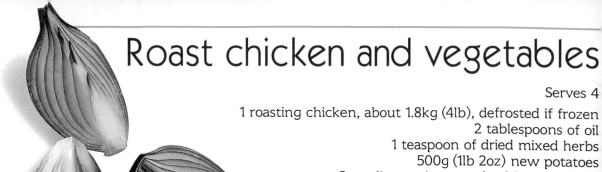

Roast chicken and vegetables

Serves 4

1 roasting chicken, about 1.8kg (4lb), defrosted if frozen
2 tablespoons of oil
1 teaspoon of dried mixed herbs
500g (1lb 2oz) new potatoes
2 medium onions, preferably red onions
1 red pepper
1 green or yellow pepper
2 tablespoons of crème fraîche or double cream
salt and ground black pepper

Heat your oven to 190°C, 375°F, Gas mark 5.

Scrub the potatoes first if they are not clean.

1. Turn on your oven. Untie the legs of the chicken. Either pull off, or cut out, the fatty pads inside the chicken's body.

2. Place the chicken in a roasting tin. Rub a tablespoon of oil over the skin. Sprinkle it with herbs and some salt and pepper.

3. Put the potatoes into a clean plastic bag. Add a tablespoon of oil. Rub the potatoes so that they become coated with oil.

Don't cut the bottom off the onions.

4. Tip the potatoes into the tin, around the chicken. Put the chicken into the oven and cook it for 45 minutes.

5. Meanwhile, cut the onions in quarters and peel off their skin. Cut the peppers into quarters and cut out the core and seeds.

6. Toss the onion and pepper pieces in the oily plastic bag. Add them to the tin when the chicken has cooked for 45 minutes.

7. So that the chicken browns evenly, put it back into the oven the other way around. Cook it for another 45 minutes.

8. After 45 minutes, scoop out the vegetables and put them in a serving dish. Put the dish into the oven, with the heat turned off.

9. Poke a knife into the meat beside a leg, to see if it is cooked. There should be no pink. If there is, cook it for five to ten more minutes.

Push a large spoon inside the chicken to lift it.

Pour the creamy juices over the pieces of chicken.

10. Lift up the chicken and hold it over the roasting tin and let the juices drip into it. Then put the chicken onto a plate.

11. Turn a ring onto a low heat and put the tin on top. Cook the juices for a minute, then stir in the crème fraîche or cream.

12. Pull the legs and thighs off the chicken and cut the rest of the meat off with a sharp knife. Serve it with the vegetables.

Lemon and honey cheesecake

Serves 6

250g (9oz) digestive biscuits
125g (4oz) butter
135g (4¾oz) packet of lemon jelly
2 tablespoons of clear honey
300g (10oz) of single cream
200g (7oz) fromage frais or quark

You will also need a 20cm (8in) flan tin with a loose base. It should be about 3cm (1½in) deep.

Use the back of a spoon to press the crumbs.

1. Put the biscuits into a clean plastic bag. Seal the bag with an elastic band. Roll a rolling pin over the biscuits to crush them.

2. Melt the butter in a saucepan over a low heat. Pour in the biscuit crumbs from the bag and mix them with the butter.

3. Grease inside of the flan tin with some butter. Spread the crumbs over the bottom. Press them to make a firm base.

4. Put the base into a fridge to chill. Use kitchen scissors to snip the jelly into cubes. Put them into a measuring jug.

5. Warm a tablespoon under a hot tap (see tip, below). Dry it and add two tablespoons of honey to the jelly cubes.

6. Pour 300ml (½ pint) of boiling water into the jug. Stir the mixture well, until the jelly dissolves. Leave the mixture to cool.

7. Meanwhile, put the cream into a large bowl. Use a wooden spoon to beat in the fromage frais or quark until it is smooth.

8. When the jelly mixture is cool, pour it into the bowl with the creamy mixture. Beat it hard with a whisk to mix it well.

9. Pour the creamy mixture into the flan tin. Put it carefully into the fridge and leave it for about four hours to set.

Measuring honey

10. When the cheesecake is firm, lift it onto a can. Carefully press down on the sides of the flan tin to loosen the base.

11. Leave the cheesecake on the tin's base. Put it onto a plate and leave it in a fridge until you are ready to eat it.

Warm your spoon under a hot tap before you dip it into a jar of honey. This makes it easier to measure.

Fudgey fruit crumble

Serves 4

500g (1lb 2oz) eating apples
6 tablespoons of water
ground mixed spice
1 tablespoon of caster sugar

For the topping: 100g (4oz) plain flour
100g (4oz) wholemeal flour
100g (4oz) sunflower margarine or butter
90g (3oz) light soft brown sugar or Demerara sugar

Heat your oven to 180°C, 350°F, Gas mark 4.

1. Cut the apples into quarters, peel them then cut out the cores. Cut the quarters into chunks. Put them in a medium pie dish.

2. Add the water. Sprinkle the apples with a large pinch of mixed spice and a tablespoon of caster sugar. Turn on your oven.

3. Stir the two kinds of flour together in a bowl. Cut the margarine or butter into small pieces and add it to the flour.

4. Wash your hands and dry them well. Rub in the margarine or butter into the flour using your fingers (see the tip, right).

5. When the mixture looks like coarse breadcrumbs, mix in the brown sugar. Mix it in with your fingers too.

6. Sprinkle the topping over the apple. Spread it out and smooth it with the back of a fork. Put the dish onto a baking tray.

Wear oven gloves.

7. Bake the crumble for 45 minutes, until the top is golden. Turn the crumble around halfway through, so that it browns evenly.

8. Push the tip of a knife into a piece of apple. If it's not soft, put the crumble back into the oven for five more minutes.

9. Leave the crumble for at least five minutes to cool a little before you serve it. Serve it with cream or ice cream.

You could use plums or blackberries instead of apples.

Rubbing in

Use a blunt knife to mix the pieces of margarine or butter. Stir and cut the flour until the pieces are coated with flour.

Rub the pieces between your fingertips. As you rub, lift the mixture up and let it drop. It will mix to look like breadcrumbs.

Strawberry trifle

Serves 4

500g (1lb) fresh strawberries
6 trifle sponges
2 tablespoons of raspberry or strawberry jam
4 tablespoons of apple juice
1 small lemon
300ml (½ pint) double cream
3 tablespoons of milk
half a teaspoon of vanilla essence
2 tablespoons of caster sugar

1. Pull the stalks out of the strawberries. Try to pull them out with the white core attached. Use a small knife to help you.

Leave a few strawberries for the top of your trifle.

2. Cut most of the strawberries in half, or in quarters if they are big. Put the pieces into a medium-sized bowl.

3. Cut the sponges in half. Spread each half with jam then press them back together again. Cut the sponges into quarters.

Grate just the skin, not the white part beneath.

4. Put the pieces of sponge on top of the strawberries and mix them gently. Trickle the apple juice over them.

5. Cover your bowl with plastic foodwrap and put it into your fridge for about three hours. The sponges will go soft.

6. Grate the yellow skin, or zest, from the lemon, using the medium holes on a grater. Use a knife to scrape off the zest.

Spread the cream with the back of a spoon.

7. When the sponge mixture is nearly chilled, put the cream into a large bowl. Add the milk, lemon zest, vanilla and sugar.

8. Beat the mixture with a whisk until it becomes slightly stiff. If you beat it too much, it will become too solid to spread.

9. Lightly spread the creamy mixture over the sponges and strawberries. Put it in the fridge until you are ready to serve it.

Gooey chocolate fudge cake

Serves 6-8

2 teaspoons of sunflower oil
250g (8oz) self-raising flour
6 tablespoons of cocoa powder
2 teaspoons of baking powder
300g (10oz) sunflower margarine
(not low fat spread)
300g (10oz) soft brown sugar

2 teaspoons of vanilla essence
6 large eggs
150g (5oz) dark chocolate
150ml (¼ pint) double cream

two 20cm (8in) round cake tins

Heat your oven to 170°C,
325°F, Gas mark 3.

Cut just inside the line you have drawn.

Use a pastry brush.

1. Turn on your oven. Put the cake tins onto baking parchment or greaseproof paper and draw around them. Cut out the circles.

2. Brush sunflower oil over the inside of the tins. Put a paper circle inside each one and brush the top of it with oil.

3. Sift the flour, cocoa and baking powder into a bowl (see page 4). Put another large bowl onto a damp dishcloth.

Use a wooden spoon.

Don't forget to add a tablespoon of flour with each egg.

This cake is best if it is eaten on the day you make it.

4. Put the margarine and sugar into the empty bowl and beat them until they are creamy. Add the vanilla and beat it again.

5. Crack one egg into a cup. Add it to the bowl with one tablespoon of flour. Beat it well. Repeat this with each egg.

Change to a metal spoon.

Spread the top level with a knife.

6. Gently stir in the rest of the flour, moving the spoon in the shape of a number eight. This keeps the mixture light.

7. Put the mixture into the cake tins. Put them on the middle shelf of the oven. Cook for 40 to 45 minutes. Test them (see page 45).

Put the cakes on wire racks to cool.

Run the knife around the edge again if it doesn't come out.

8. Wear oven gloves to lift the tins from the oven. Let them cool for five minutes, then run a knife around the sides of each tin.

9. Turn each tin upside down over a wire rack and shake it. The cakes should pop out. Peel off the paper and leave them to cool.

10. For the icing, break the chocolate into a heatproof bowl. Add the cream. Heat 5cm (2in) of water in a pan until it is just bubbling.

Put the cake on a plate.

11. Put the bowl in the pan. Stir the chocolate as it melts. When it has melted, let it cool, then put it into the fridge.

12. Stir the icing a few times while it is cooling in the fridge. It will thicken. When it is like soft butter, take it out of the fridge.

13. Spread a third of the icing on one cake. Put the other cake on top of it and cover the top and sides with your icing.

Carrot cake

Serves 8-12 slices

a little oil for greasing
250g (9oz) carrots
150g (5oz) margarine
200g (7oz) light soft brown sugar
2 large eggs
200g (7oz) self-raising flour
half a teaspoon of salt
2 teaspoons of ground cinnamon
2 teaspoons of baking powder

125g (4¼ oz) raisins
75g (2¾ oz) chopped walnuts
2 tablespoons of milk

For the topping: 200g (7oz) cream cheese
1 tablespoon of lemon juice
50g (2oz) icing sugar
half a teaspoon of vanilla essence

a 20cm (8in) round cake tin

Heat your oven to 180°C, 350°F, Gas mark 4.

Cut just inside the line.

1. Put your cake tin onto a piece of baking parchment or greaseproof paper and draw around it. Cut out the circle.

2. Brush the sides and the base of tin with a little oil to grease it. Put the paper circle inside and brush this with oil, too.

3. Turn your oven on. Wash the carrots and cut off their tops. Grate them on the side of the grater with the biggest holes.

Put the bowl on a damp cloth.

4. Put the margarine into a saucepan and heat it slowly until it has just melted. Pour it into a large bowl.

5. Break the eggs into a small bowl and beat them. Stir the carrots and sugar into the margarine. Then, add the beaten eggs.

6. Put a sieve over the bowl. Shake the flour, salt, cinnamon and baking powder through the sieve, onto the mixture.

Push it in the middle.

7. Use a wooden spoon to beat the mixture, until it is smooth. Mix in the raisins and walnuts, then stir in the milk.

8. Spoon the mixture into the tin. Smooth the top with a spoon. Tap the tin on your work surface to make the mixture level.

9. Bake the cake for an hour. Test it by sticking a skewer into it. When it comes out it should have no mixture sticking to it.

10. Put the cake tin on a wire rack and leave it for ten minutes. Then, run a knife around the side of the cake.

11. Hold the rack on top of the tin and turn them both over. Shake the tin gently to get the cake out. Peel off the paper.

12. While the cake is cooling, sift the icing sugar into a bowl. Add the cheese, lemon juice and vanilla.

Testing a cake

13. Beat the mixture well. When the cake has cooled completely, cut it in half. Spread one piece with half of the topping.

14. Put the other half of the cake on top. Spread the top of it with topping Make swirly patterns on it with a fork.

Push a skewer or a sharp knife into the middle of the cake. If the cake is cooked, it will come out clean.

Tasty cookies

Makes about 60 cookies. This recipe shows you how to make fruit cookies. See the labels for other flavours.

200g (7oz) plain flour
quarter of a teaspoon of salt
2 teaspoons of baking powder
1 large egg
150g (5oz) butter
200g (7oz) caster sugar
1 teaspoon of vanilla essence
1 orange and 1 lemon

You can add all kinds of things to these cookies. Try 50g (2oz) of chopped hazelnuts instead of the orange and lemon zest.

Heat your oven to 200°C, 400°F, Gas mark 6.

1. Weigh the butter and leave it for about an hour to soften. Sift the flour, salt and baking powder into a bowl (see page 4).

2. Break the egg into a cup. Beat it briskly with a fork, so that the yolk and the white are mixed well together.

3. Put the butter and sugar into another bowl and beat them until they are creamy. Stir in the egg and vanilla essence.

Scrape the zest off the grater with a knife.

4. Grate the skin, or zest, off the orange and lemon using the medium holes on your grater. Stir it into the creamy mixture.

Orange and lemon cookies.

5. Add the flour and stir it until you get a smooth dough. If the dough feels very soft, put it into your fridge for an hour.

6. Put a long piece of foil onto your work surface and scrape the dough onto it. Roll the dough to make a long sausage shape.

For chocolate cookies, add two tablespoons of cocoa powder. Sift it in with the flour.

Use four tablespoons of desiccated coconut instead of the zest to make coconut cookies.

7. Wrap the foil around the dough and put it in your fridge for about an hour, until it becomes firm. Turn on your oven.

8. Take the dough out of the fridge and cut it into very thin slices. You don't need to use all the dough at one time (see the tip).

Storing the dough

9. Spread out the slices of dough on a non-stick baking sheet. Bake them for about seven minutes, until they are golden.

10. Leave the cookies on the baking sheet for a minute. Use a fish slice to slide them onto a wire rack to cool.

Wrap any spare dough in foil. It will keep for about ten days in a fridge or up to six weeks in a freezer.

Weights and measures

For a recipe to work well, it's important to measure the ingredients accurately. Here are a few tips to help you.

• When you measure a liquid, look at the mark on your measuring cup at eye level, not from above.

• If you're using a spoon to measure, make sure that the ingredient is level with the edge of the spoon and not heaped up.

• If you are measuring something like herbs, a liquid or salt in a spoon, don't hold the spoon over the mixture you are cooking, just in case some spills out of the spoon and into the mixture.

• If you don't have a tablespoon you can use a teaspoon instead. Three teaspoons is the same as one tablespoon.

Measuring liquids and solids

These conversions are equivalent measurements which are easy to use when you are cooking. They are not exact conversions.

Liquids		
Spoons	cups	fluid ounces
3 teaspoons	$1/8$ cup	
1 tablespoon	15ml	½floz
2 tablespoons	25ml	1floz
4 tablespoons	50ml	2floz
8 tablespoons	75ml	4floz
¼ pint	150ml	5floz
½ pint	300ml	10floz
¾ pint	450ml	15floz
1 pint	600ml	20floz
1¾ pints	1 litre	35floz

Solids	
Grammes	ounces/pounds
25g	1oz
50g	2oz
75g	3oz
125g	4oz
150g	5oz
175g	6oz
225g	8oz
350g	12oz
400g	14oz
450g	16oz (1lb)

Oven temperatures

Electric ovens		Gas ovens
Celsius	Fahrenheit	Mark
110°C	225°F	¼
130°C	250°F	½
140°C	275°F	1
150°C	300°F	2
170°C	325°F	3
180°C	350°F	4

Electric ovens		Gas ovens
Celsius	Fahrenheit	Mark
190°C	375°F	5
200°C	400°F	6
220°C	425°F	7
230°C	450°F	8
240°C	475°F	9

PASTA & PIZZA

FOR BEGINNERS

Successful cooking

Before you cook any of the pasta or pizza recipes in this part of the book, read the tips on these two pages. Check that you have all the ingredients before your start. Don't worry if you haven't got the type or shape of pasta suggested in the recipe. Look on page 96, where you will find some alternative types to use.

Things to remember

The ingredients' lists show both grammes and ounces for measuring. Follow the recipe using one or the other, but don't mix them up. All the recipes tell you how long to cook the ingredients, so follow these closely. Don't forget that if you have a fan oven look at its instruction book. Either, shorten the cooking time or turn down the temperature by the amount it says.

Pizza bases

On pages 78-79 and 82-83, there are recipes for two different kinds of pizza bases. If you don't have time to make a base, many supermarkets sell ready-made bases. If you use one, just make the pizza topping from the recipe. You can also buy mixes for pizza bases.

Chopping onions

1. Put the onion onto a chopping board and use a vegetable knife to chop off the top and the roots. Take care as you cut.

2. Slice through the papery outside skin. Use a fingernail to lift the skin at the slice then peel the rest of the skin away.

3. Cut the onion in half. Lay the flat side on your chopping board and holding the onion firmly, slice it as finely as you can.

Garlic

A garlic bulb

A clove of garlic

You may need to use a knife to split the skin.

If your recipe uses garlic, it will tell you how many cloves you will need. A clove is one part of a whole bulb of garlic.

1. Squeeze and twist the garlic bulb so that the the outer skin breaks. Pull a clove of garlic off the bottom of the stem.

2. Cut a small piece off the top and bottom of the clove, then peel off the skin. The clove is now ready to use.

Fresh or dried pasta?

You can use fresh or dried pasta for all the pasta dishes. You will need a different amount depending on the type you use. See the ingredients' lists.

Mushrooms

Cut the end off the stalk.

Don't wash mushrooms before you use them but wipe them clean with a damp paper towel.

Mozzarella cheese

The pizza recipes use two types of mozzarella cheese. If it says to use 'mozzarella cheese', use the kind you buy in a plastic bag, surrounded by liquid. The other kind is written as 'grated mozzarella'. You can buy this ready-grated or as a large solid block.

Mozzarella cheese is soft and you can't grate it. Slit the bag you buy it in and pour away the liquid, before you slice it.

Grated mozzarella is firmer than the other kind. Some supermarkets sell it as 'pizza cheese'.

Types of pasta

Each of the pasta recipes suggests a type of pasta for you to cook, but in most cases you can use any shape you like (see page 96). Most supermarkets sell lots of different kinds of fresh and dried pasta. If you see the words 'rigate' on a packet of pasta, it just means that it has a ridged surface.

Tagliarini. Tagliatelle is like this but is thicker.

Macaroni (tubes)

Tortellini (little twists). These are often stuffed with spinach, cheese or meat.

Ravioli. These are usually filled with meat but sometimes with vegetables, fish or cheese.

Fusilli (spirals)

Conchigliette (little shells)

Conchiglie giganti

Conchiglie (shells)

Penne (quills)

Egg noodles

Cooking pasta

The amount of time you need to cook pasta depends on its type and shape. Fresh pasta and long thin shapes cook more quickly than dried pasta or chunky shapes. Try not to overcook your pasta. It should be firm, not soggy.

Make the pan three-quarters full.

Oil stops the pasta from sticking.

1. Fill a very large saucepan with water. Turn on the heat and bring the water to boil. While the water is heating, weigh your pasta on some kitchen scales.

2. When the water is boiling and the surface looks as if it is 'rolling', not just bubbling, add a teaspoon of salt and a tablespoon of cooking oil.

3. Add the pasta to the pan and stir it to separate it. When you add the pasta the water will stop boiling. Turn up the heat and bring it to boiling again.

Turn down the heat if the water looks as if it will boil over.

4. Start to time your cooking, following the instructions on the packet of pasta, from when the water boils with the pasta in it.

5. When the pasta has cooked for the correct time, hold a colander over a sink and pour the pasta into it. You may need help to hold the pan.

6. If you need to leave your pasta in a colander, put a little butter on it. Toss the pasta so that it is coated. Put a plate on top to keep it warm.

Cooking spaghetti

Vermicelli (little worms)

Red pasta has tomato in it and green pasta is made with spinach.

Spaghetti

Farfalle (butterflies)

When you cook dried spaghetti, hold one end and gently press it into the water as it softens. Use a spoon to press the ends under the water.

Spaghetti alla carbonara

Serves 4

375g (12oz) dried spaghetti,
   or 450g (15oz) fresh spaghetti

For the sauce: 200g (8oz) streaky bacon or ham
1 large onion
2 cloves of garlic
1 tablespoon of cooking oil
3 eggs
3 tablespoons of single cream
ground black pepper
40g (1½oz) grated Parmesan cheese
40g (1½oz) butter
1 level tablespoon of chopped parsley

Add the spaghetti when the water is boiling.

Stir the onion and garlic as they are cooking.

1. Peel and chop the onion. Snip the rind off the bacon and cut the rashers in strips 1cm (½in) wide. Peel and crush the garlic (see right).

2. Read the instructions on the packet of spaghetti to find out how long it will take to cook. Weigh it and start to cook it.

3. Heat the oil gently in a frying pan. Add the onion and garlic, and cook them for about five minutes until they are soft.

Stir the mixture as it is cooking.

Turn off the heat when you drain the spaghetti.

4. Add the bacon or ham. If you are using bacon, cook it until it is brown and crispy. If you are using ham, cook it until it is hot.

5. Use a fork to beat the eggs, cream, a pinch of black pepper and most of the cheese to make a creamy mixture.

6. When the spaghetti is cooked, drain it then put it back into the pan. Add the butter and toss the spaghetti until it is coated.

The heat from the spaghetti cooks the egg.

7. Add the bacon, onion and garlic then stir in the cheesy mixture. Use a fork to toss the spaghetti quickly, until it is coated.

8. Put the spaghetti onto four plates or bowls. Sprinkle on the parsley and the rest of the cheese. Serve immediately.

Crushing garlic

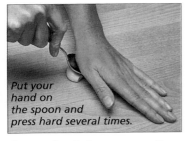

Put your hand on the spoon and press hard several times.

If you don't have a garlic crusher, put a clove of garlic on a chopping board. Put the back of a spoon onto it and press down.

Garlic mushroom pasta

Serves 4

400g (14oz) dried fusilli,
  or 500g (1lb) fresh fusilli

For the sauce: 75g (3oz) butter
450g (1lb) mushrooms
1 clove of garlic
salt and ground black pepper
200g (7oz) crème fraîche

1. Fill a pan with water and bring it to the boil. Weigh your pasta and add it to the pan. Leave it cooking.

2. Slice the mushrooms thinly. Peel and crush the garlic. Gently melt the butter in a pan. Add the mushrooms and garlic.

3. Add a pinch of salt and pepper to the pan and cook the mixture for about five minutes, stirring occasionally.

Serve your pasta on plates or in large, flat bowls.

4. Drain the pasta and add it to the mushrooms. Add the crème fraîche and stir it until it melts. Serve immediately.

This three-coloured pasta is called 'tricolori fusilli'.

Spicy sausage pasta

Serves 4

400g (14oz) dried conchiglie,
   or 500g (1lb) fresh conchiglie

For the sauce: 2 tablespoons of olive oil
1 onion
1 clove of garlic
400g (14oz) can of chopped tomatoes
4 chorizo sausages
1 tablespoon of chopped parsley

1. Peel the onion and slice
it finely. Peel and crush
the clove of garlic. Put the
oil in a large pan and heat
it gently.

The sauce
will
reduce in
amount.

2. Add the onion and
garlic. Cook them for five
minutes or until the onion
is soft. Stir the mixture as
it is cooking.

3. Add the tomatoes to
the pan and bring it to
boil. Turn the heat down
and let the sauce bubble
gently for 20 minutes.

*Chorizo sausages are very
spicy. Use kabanos sausages
or salami if you don't like
spicy food.*

4. While the sauce is
cooking, put a pan of
water on to boil. Cook the
pasta following the
instructions on its packet.

5. Cut the ends off the
sausages. Peel the papery
skin off the sausages. Slice
each sausage and add the
slices to the sauce.

6. Drain the pasta and
divide it between four
bowls or plates. Spoon the
sauce on top and sprinkle
with parsley.

Macaroni cheese

Serves 4.

175g (6oz) dried macaroni,
  or 200g (7oz) fresh macaroni

For the cheese sauce:
50g (2oz) margarine or butter
50g (2oz) plain flour
600ml (1 pint) milk
1 teaspoon of mustard paste
175g (6oz) Cheddar cheese, grated
salt and pepper

For the topping:
25g (1oz) Cheddar cheese, grated

Heat your oven to 180°C, 350°F, Gas mark 4.

Put the macaroni back into the pan after you have drained it.

Use a wooden spoon to stir.

1. Turn on your oven. Weigh the macaroni. Read the instructions on its packet and cook it for the time it says. Drain it.

2. To make the sauce, melt the margarine or butter in a pan over a low heat. Stir in the flour and cook it for one minute.

3. Take your pan off the heat and add a little milk. Stir it really well. Carry on stirring in the rest of the milk, a little at a time.

Add a pinch of salt and pepper too.

4. Return your pan to the heat and start to bring it to boil, stirring all the time. The sauce will stick if you don't stir it.

5. The sauce will begin to thicken. Let the sauce bubble for a minute then turn off the heat. Stir in the mustard and cheese.

6. Pour the sauce over the cooked macaroni. Stir it well so that the sauce coats all of the pieces of macaroni.

7. Dip a paper towel into some margarine and rub it inside an ovenproof dish to grease it. Pour in the cheesy macaroni.

8. Sprinkle grated cheese on top. Put the dish into the oven for about 25 minutes, until the top is golden brown.

Add the cheese to a sauce after you have turned off the heat and the sauce coats the back of your spoon when you lift it.

Penne with Bolognese sauce

Serves 4

400g (14oz) dried penne,
  or 500g (1lb) fresh penne

For the sauce: 2 tablespoons of olive oil
2 rashers of streaky bacon
1 onion
1 carrot
1 stick of celery
1 clove of garlic
225g (8oz) lean minced beef or lamb
225g (8oz) can of chopped tomatoes
2 tablespoons of tomato purée
1 beef or vegetable stock cube
1 teaspoon of dried basil
freshly ground black pepper

To serve: grated Parmesan cheese

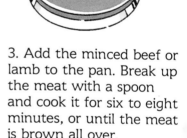

1. Peel or scrape the carrot then grate it. Crush the garlic and chop the bacon, onion and celery finely. Heat the oil in a saucepan over a medium heat.

2. Add the bacon to the pan and cook for three or four minutes. Stir it occasionally. Add all the vegetables and cook them until they are soft.

3. Add the minced beef or lamb to the pan. Break up the meat with a spoon and cook it for six to eight minutes, or until the meat is brown all over.

4. Boil a kettle of water. Crumble the stock cube into a measuring jug and pour in 125ml (4floz) of water. Stir it well then add it to the meat.

5. Pour in the tomatoes. Stir in the purée and basil. Put a lid on and let the sauce bubble gently for 30-40 minutes. Remove the lid halfway through.

6. As the sauce is cooking, stir it occasionally to stop it from sticking. It will become thicker and the amount of liquid will reduce.

Making stock

7. About 15 minutes before the sauce is ready, boil a pan of water. Add the pasta and cook for the time it says on its packet. Drain it and serve immediately.

1. Boil a kettle. Either cut up or crumble a stock cube and put it into a measuring jug.

2. Pour in the amount of water you need for your recipe. Stir it well until the stock cube dissolves.

Spoon the sauce over the hot penne and sprinkle with Parmesan cheese.

Pasta with green vegetables

Serves 4

375g (12oz) dried tagliarini
  or 400g (14oz) fresh tagliarini
25g (1oz) butter
 4 spring onions
    225g (8oz) broccoli
      125g (4oz) fine green beans
      125g (4oz) mangetout
        1 courgette
          250g (8oz) soft cheese with
            garlic and herbs

This green and yellow tagliarini is known as 'paglia e fieno' (straw and hay).

1. Chop the top and bottom off the spring onions. Pull off the outer layer. Cut them into pieces, 3cm (1in) long.

2. Use a knife to cut the curly ends off the broccoli stalks. Trim the ends off the green beans and cut them in half.

Cut the courgette in half across the middle, not lengthways.

3. Trim the ends off the mangetout. Chop them in half. Cut the ends off the courgette and cut it in half. Slice it into thin strips.

Cook on a low heat.

4. Fill a pan with water and boil it. Add the broccoli and beans and cook them for three minutes. Drain them.

5. Boil a pan of water for the pasta. Melt the butter in a frying pan. Add the onion, broccoli and beans. Cook them for five minutes.

6. Add the rest of the vegetables. Cook them for a further three minutes, stirring them occasionally.

Stir in a little milk if the sauce seems too thick.

Trimming vegetables

7. Cook the pasta for three minutes then drain it. Put it back into the pan and add the vegetables. Mix them well.

8. Add the cheese. Break it up with a spoon. Cook over a low heat until the cheese melts. Serve it immediately.

It's easier to use scissors rather than a knife to trim vegetables like beans or mangetout.

Ravioli with tomato sauce

Serves 4

400g (14oz) fresh, or 400g (14oz) dried ravioli
1 tablespoon of olive oil
1 onion
1 clove of garlic
400g (14oz) can of chopped tomatoes
salt and black pepper
8 basil leaves
125g (4oz) mozzarella cheese

This sauce is tasty with ravioli filled with meat, cheese or fish.

1. Peel the onion and chop it finely. Peel and crush the garlic. Heat the oil in a saucepan and add the onion and garlic.

2. When the onion and garlic are soft, add some salt and pepper and the tomatoes. Let it bubble gently for 15 minutes.

3. While the sauce is cooking, cut the cheese and basil into thin strips. Boil a pan of water for the ravioli.

4. When the water for the pasta is boiling, add the ravioli and cook it, following the instructions on its packet.

5. Just before the pasta is ready, add the cheese and basil to the sauce. Let the cheese melt a little then serve immediately.

Cheesy tortellini

Serves 4

400g (14oz) fresh tortellini
50g (2oz) butter
200ml (7fl oz) double cream
150ml (¼ pint) milk
175g (6oz) Cheddar or Gruyère cheese
1 heaped tablespoon of chopped parsley

Stir it as it cooks.

1. Grate the cheese. Boil a pan of water. Add the tortellini and cook them following the instructions on their packet.

2. Put the butter, cream, milk and cheese into a pan and heat them gently for about five minutes, until the cheese melts.

3. Let the cheese sauce bubble gently for five minutes, stirring it from time to time. Add the chopped parsley.

4. Drain the pasta well and pour it into the cheese sauce. Stir it so that the pasta is coated then eat it immediately.

Spinach and ricotta pasta shells

Serves 4

16 conchiglie giganti (giant pasta shells)

For the filling: 1 onion
1 tablespoon of olive oil
1 clove of garlic
225g (8oz) fresh spinach
225g (8oz) ricotta cheese

For the tomato sauce: 1 onion
1 tablespoon of oil
1 clove of garlic
1 level tablespoon of tomato purée
2 level teaspoons of sugar
400g (14oz) can of chopped tomatoes
1 tablespoon of fresh chopped basil
salt and black pepper

To serve: grated Parmesan cheese

You can use 175g (6oz) of frozen spinach instead of fresh. Thaw it and drain it well. You don't need to add any water when you heat it at step 4.

1. Fill a large pan with water and bring it to boil. Add the pasta shells and cook them according to their packet.

2. While the pasta is cooking, start to make the filling. Peel the onion and chop it very finely. Peel and crush the garlic.

3. Heat the oil and cook the onion and garlic until they are soft, but don't let them go brown. Spoon them into a mixing bowl.

Stir it as it cooks.

4. Wash the spinach well. Put it into a large pan and cook it over a medium heat for about two minutes.

5. Spoon the spinach into a colander. Press it with the back of a large spoon to squeeze out as much liquid as you can.

6. Put the spinach onto a chopping board and cut it up into small pieces. Use a fork to hold it as it will still be hot.

Toss the pasta in a little butter.

Make the sauce in a big, shallow pan.

7. When the shells are cooked, drain them in a colander and leave them to cool a little. Carry on making the filling.

8. Put the spinach into the bowl along with the ricotta. Add a pinch of salt and pepper and mix everything together.

9. Make the tomato sauce following steps 2 to 5 on page 81. While the sauce is bubbling, begin to fill the pasta shells.

10. Hold the shell in one hand and use a teaspoon to fill each shell with some of the spinach and ricotta mixture.

11. When all the shells are filled, lay them, open-side up into the sauce. Heat them for 10-15 minutes with a lid on top.

12. Spoon four shells and some sauce onto each plate. Sprinkle them with Parmesan cheese and eat them immediately.

Chicken and bacon pasta

Serves 4

400g (14oz) dried tagliatelle,
   or 500g (1 lb) fresh tagliatelle

50g (2oz) margarine or butter
450g (14oz) chicken, without
   any bones
4 rashers of bacon
100g (4oz) mushrooms
4 spring onions
1 teaspoon of chopped parsley
2 level tablespoons of flour
300ml (½ pint) milk
4 heaped tablespoons of crème fraîche
salt and ground black pepper

Cook over a low heat.

Use kitchen scissors to cut the bacon.

1. Cut the roots off each spring onion. Trim the top and peel off the outer layer. Cut them into 2cm (1in) pieces.

2. Slice the mushrooms finely. Snip any rind off the bacon then cut the rashers into pieces. Put a pan of water on to boil.

3. Chop the chicken into small chunks. Melt the margarine or butter in another saucepan and stir in the chopped chicken.

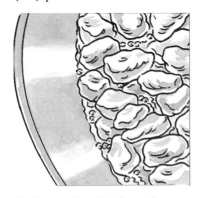

4. Cook the chicken for five minutes until it loses its pinkness. Cut one piece in half to check that it's cooked right through.

5. Add the bacon to the chicken and cook for three minutes more. Then add the mushrooms and onions to the pan.

6. Cook the mixture for two minutes then stir in the flour. Cook it for a minute then take the pan off the heat.

The sauce will take about a minute to thicken.

7. Gradually add the milk, stirring it all the time. Put the pan back on the heat and let it bubble gently until the sauce thickens.

8. Add the crème fraîche and parsley. Put in a pinch of salt and pepper. Turn the heat as low as it will go while you cook the pasta.

9. Cook the pasta, following the time on its packet. Drain it and put it back into its pan. Stir in the sauce. Eat it immediately.

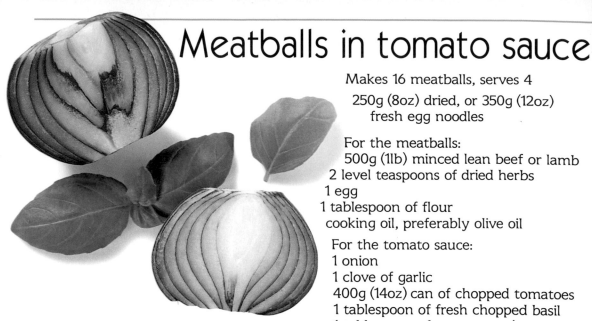

Meatballs in tomato sauce

Makes 16 meatballs, serves 4

250g (8oz) dried, or 350g (12oz)
fresh egg noodles

For the meatballs:
500g (1lb) minced lean beef or lamb
2 level teaspoons of dried herbs
1 egg
1 tablespoon of flour
cooking oil, preferably olive oil

For the tomato sauce:
1 onion
1 clove of garlic
400g (14oz) can of chopped tomatoes
1 tablespoon of fresh chopped basil
1 tablespoon of tomato purée
salt and ground black pepper

Use a large mixing bowl.

1. Put the meat into a bowl and break it up with a fork. Crack the egg into a cup then add it, along with the mixed herbs and flour.

2. Wash your hands. Pick up some of the mixture and shape it into a ball, about the size of a table tennis ball. Make 15 more.

3. Heat three tablespoons of oil in a frying pan and add eight meatballs. Turn them often, until they are brown all over.

Always keep raw meat and cooked meat apart.

Stir the onion and garlic as they cook.

4. Put a paper towel onto a plate and lift the browned meatballs onto it. Brown the other eight meatballs and put them on the plate.

5. Chop the onion and peel and crush the garlic. Heat a tablespoon of oil in a saucepan and fry them until they are soft.

6. Add the tomatoes, basil, purée and salt and pepper. Let it boil, then turn down the heat and bubble it gently for ten minutes.

You may have to look in the Oriental food section in your supermarket to find egg noodles. You could use spaghetti or vermicelli instead.

The oil prevents the noodles from sticking together.

Cook the noodles when the meatballs are ready.

7. Add the meatballs. Put a lid onto the pan and leave the sauce to bubble gently for 20 minutes, stirring occasionally.

8. While the meatballs are cooking, half-fill a pan with water and bring it to the boil. Add a tablespoon of oil to the water.

9. Add the noodles, let the water boil again, then simmer for the time it says on their packet. Drain and serve with the meatballs.

Minestrone soup

Serves 4

4 rashers of bacon or pancetta
2 sticks of celery
2 medium-sized potatoes
2 carrots
1 onion
1 leek
1 clove of garlic
1 tablespoon of cooking oil, preferably olive oil
1 tablespoon of tomato purée
2 stock cubes
1.2 litres (2 pints) of water
1 teaspoon of mixed dried herbs
a quarter of a small dark green cabbage
50g (2oz) small dried pasta shapes
50g (2oz) frozen peas
salt and ground black pepper

To serve: 50g (2oz) grated Parmesan cheese

Instead of using pasta shapes, you could use spaghetti broken into small pieces.

1. Use a clean pair of kitchen scissors to remove the rind from the bacon. Snip the rashers into strips about 2cm (¾ in) wide.

2. Peel the potatoes and cut them in half. Cut each piece into 1cm (½ in) slices. Then cut the slices into cubes.

3. Wash the celery and the leek, and peel the carrots. Cut them all into thin slices. Peel the garlic. Peel the onion and slice it.

4. Heat the oil in a saucepan. Add the bacon. Cook it for a few minutes until it is brown then crush the garlic into the pan.

5. Add all the vegetables you have chopped and stir them well. Let them cook for five minutes, stirring them often.

6. Crumble the stock cube into a measuring jug and pour in 600ml (1 pint) of boiling water. Add the tomato purée and stir well.

Cut out the stalk before you slice it.

7. Pour the stock mixture into the pan, Add another 600ml (1 pint) of water, along with the herbs and a pinch of salt and pepper.

8. Turn up the heat so that the mixture boils. Put a lid on the pan and let the sauce bubble gently for about 20 minutes.

9. Meanwhile, remove the outer leaves from the quarter of cabbage and wash it. Cut it into very thin slices.

10. Add the cabbage and pasta to the pan and let it boil. Turn the heat down and cover it. Cook it for ten more minutes.

11. Add the peas to the pan and stir them in well. Let the soup cook for another two minutes until the peas have heated up.

12. Use a ladle to spoon the soup into four bowls. Sprinkle a little Parmesan cheese on top of the soup and eat it immediately.

Stir fry with vermicelli

Serves 4

175g (6oz) dried vermicelli,
   or 225g (8oz) fresh vermicelli
3 tablespoons of soy sauce
1 tablespoon of lemon juice
1 tablespoon of clear honey
3cm (1in) piece of fresh ginger
285g (10oz) boneless chicken breast
2 carrots
1 red pepper
1 clove of garlic
100g (4oz) mangetout
100g (4oz) baby sweetcorn
100g (4oz) mushrooms
4 spring onions
1 tablespoon of sunflower oil
a vegetable stock cube

1. Cut the light brown skin off the piece of ginger. Cut the ginger into thin slices, then cut the slices into very thin strips.

2. Put the soy sauce, lemon juice and honey in a bowl. Add the pieces of ginger and stir them well. This is your marinade.

3. Cut the chicken into strips about 2cm (¾ in) wide. Add it to the marinade and stir well. Leave it for half an hour.

4. While the chicken is marinading, make 300ml (½ pint) of stock (see page 61). Peel the carrots and cut them into thin 'sticks'.

See the tip on page 89.

5. Cut the ends off the pepper. Chop it in half and cut out the seeds. Slice the pepper into thin strips. Peel and crush the garlic.

6. Cut the stalks off the mangetout and slice the top off the sweetcorn. Cut them all in quarters. Slice the mushrooms.

7. Trim the ends off the spring onions, then cut them into pieces about 3cm (1in) long. Put a pan of water on to boil.

8. Heat the oil in a frying pan. When the oil is hot, add the garlic. Spoon in the chicken, leaving your marinade in the bowl.

9. Cook the chicken for five minutes. When all the pinkness has gone, add all the vegetables to the pan.

Stir it all the time.

10. Stir the vegetables for three minutes. Pour in the stock and marinade and let it boil. Cook for two more minutes.

11. Add the vermicelli to the pan of boiling water. Boil it for three minutes, stirring occasionally then drain it well.

12. Add the vermicelli to the vegetables and stir it in. Leave the mixture for a minute then eat it immediately.

Tuna and tomato pasta salad

Serves 4

300g (10oz) dried farfalle,
or 375g (12oz) fresh farfalle
400g (14oz) can of tuna
10 cherry tomatoes
175g (6oz) thin green beans

For the dressing:
4 tablespoons of mayonnaise
4 tablespoons of milk
salt and black pepper
4 fresh chives

Toss the pasta with some butter.

1. Fill a large saucepan with water and bring it to the boil. Weigh the pasta and add it to the pan when it is boiling.

2. Cook the pasta following the instructions on its packet. Pour the pasta into a colander to drain it. Leave it to cool.

3. Use kitchen scissors to snip the ends off the beans. Cut the beans in half. Put on a pan of water to boil.

4. When the water is boiling, add the beans and cook them for five minutes. Drain them and rinse them with cold water.

5. Open the can of tuna. Tip it into a sieve to drain away the liquid. Put it on a saucer and use a fork to break it up a little.

6. Put the pasta, beans, and tuna into a large bowl and mix them. Cut the tomatoes in half and add them to the bowl.

Instead of making a dressing, you could toss your salad in a ready-made one.

7. Put the mayonnaise and milk into a bowl and add a pinch of salt and pepper. Use a fork to mix them together well.

8. Pour the dressing over the pasta mixture. Use a fork to toss the mixture in the dressing so that it is covered.

9. Use kitchen scissors to snip the chives into small pieces and scatter them over the top. Spoon the salad onto plates or bowls.

Making a pizza base

This traditional pizza dough will make a round pizza 25cm (10in) across, or a rectangular one 35 x 25cm (14 x 10in).

350g (12oz) strong plain flour
1 teaspoon of salt
15g (½oz) fresh yeast, or 1 teaspoon of easy blend yeast
200ml (7fl oz) of warm water
1 tablespoon of olive oil
margarine for greasing

Cook your pizza on a large baking sheet or on a baking tray like this.

a baking sheet or tray, about 35 x 25cm (14 x 10in)

It should take about 15 minutes to go frothy.

1. If you are using fresh yeast, mix it with a little of the warm water. Leave it in a warm place until it goes frothy.

If you are using easy blend yeast, open the packet, but don't add any warm water to it now. Add all the water at step 2.

2. Use a sieve to sift the flour and salt. Add the oil, yeast mixture and the rest of the warm water. Stir them well.

3. Carry on stirring the mixture until you get a soft dough which doesn't stick to the sides of the bowl. Wash your hands.

4. Sprinkle flour onto a clean, dry work surface and knead the dough well until it is smooth and stretchy (see right).

5. Dip a paper towel into some margarine and rub it inside a large bowl to grease it. Put the dough into the bowl.

Kneading

The dough stretches as you push it.

1. Use the heels of both hands, or your knuckles, to push the dough away.

2. Fold the dough in half and turn it around. Push it away from you again.

3. Fold and turn the dough again. Push it away from you as you did before.

4. Carry on folding, turning and pushing until the dough feels smooth and stretchy.

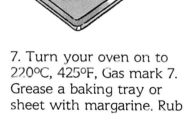

6. Cover the bowl with plastic foodwrap. Put it in a warm place for about 45 minutes, or until it has risen to twice its size.

7. Turn your oven on to 220°C, 425°F, Gas mark 7. Grease a baking tray or sheet with margarine. Rub it all over.

8. When the dough has risen, knead it again so that you burst all the large air bubbles in it. It won't take very long.

9. Put the dough onto your baking tray. Press it into the shape you want. Pinch up the edges. It's now ready for its topping.

Neapolitan pizza

Serves 6 - makes a rectangular pizza
30 x 25cm (14 x 10in)

One traditional pizza base - see pages 78-79

For the tomato sauce: 1 tablespoon of olive oil
1 onion
1 clove of garlic
1 tablespoon of tomato purée
400g (14oz) can of chopped tomatoes
2 teaspoons of sugar
1 tablespoon of fresh basil, chopped,
    or 2 teaspoons of dried basil
salt and ground black pepper

For the topping: 250g (8oz) mozzarella cheese
50g (2oz) tin of anchovy fillets
1 tablespoon of fresh basil, chopped,
    or 2 teaspoons of dried basil
50g (2oz) black olives (without their stones)

Heat your oven to 220°C, 425°F, Gas mark 7.

1. Turn on your oven. Follow pages 78-79 to make a pizza base. While the dough is rising, make the tomato sauce.

2. Chop the onion finely and crush the garlic. Put a tablespoon of oil into a medium-sized pan and heat it gently.

3. Add the onion to the pan and stir it on and off for about five minutes until it has softened. Try not to let it go brown.

4. Add the garlic, tomato purée, tomatoes, sugar, basil and a pinch of salt and pepper. Stir it and let the mixture bubble gently.

5. Leave the sauce to cook for 20 minutes or until the sauce becomes thicker and the amount has reduced.

6. When your dough has risen, grease your baking tray with margarine. Place the dough in the middle of the tray.

7. Press the dough out with your fingers to make a rectangle about 30 x 25cm (14 x 10 in). Pinch up the edges to make a rim.

8. Use a spoon to spread the tomato sauce all over the base. Slice the cheese thinly and lay the slices over the sauce.

9. Open the tin of anchovies carefully and drain out the oil. Cut each anchovy in half lengthways.

10. Lay the anchovies in diagonal lines across the pizza. Make lines the other way to make a criss-cross pattern.

11. Sprinkle the basil all over the top then put an olive in the middle of each diamond shape made by the anchovies.

12. Put the pizza into the oven to bake for about 20 minutes, until the base is crisp and golden. Serve the pizza immediately.

Quick Margherita pizza

Makes one 30cm (12in) round pizza.
This recipe uses a scone base, rather than the traditional base on pages 78-79.

For the scone base: 225g (8oz) self-raising flour
½ a teaspoon of salt
2 tablespoons of cooking oil
150ml (¼ pint) of water

For the topping: 1 tablespoon of cooking oil
2 onions
400g (14oz) can of plum tomatoes
1 teaspoon of mixed dried herbs
salt and ground black pepper
225g (8oz) mozzarella cheese

Heat your oven to 200ºC, 400ºF, Gas mark 6.

Make sure that your work surface is clean and dry, first.

1. To make the base, use a sieve to sift the flour and salt. Add the oil and water. Use a round-ended knife to mix them to make dough.

2. Grease a baking tray with margarine on a paper towel. Sprinkle flour onto your work surface. Knead the dough (see page 79).

3. Rub a little flour onto a rolling pin. Gently roll the dough, turning between each roll, into a circle about 30cm (12in) across.

Pinch up a rim around the edge.

4. Carefully lift up one edge of the dough and slide the rolling pin under it. Lift the dough onto your baking tray.

5. To make the topping, peel the onions and chop them finely. Gently heat the oil and cook the onions until they are soft.

6. While the onions are cooking, open the tin of tomatoes and drain them in a sieve. Chop them into small pieces.

This pizza is delicious eaten hot or cold.

7. Add the tomatoes and herbs to the onion. Add a pinch of salt and pepper and cook the mixture for ten minutes.

8. Use a spoon to spread the topping over the base. Cut the cheese in thin slices then lay them all over the topping.

9. Bake your pizza in the oven for 25-30 minutes. The base will rise as it cooks and the cheese will go golden.

Mini pizzas

Makes 4 pizzas 15cm (6in) across

One traditional pizza base - see pages 78-79

For the toppings: 2 slices of cooked ham
1 pineapple ring
1 tomato
2 large basil leaves
25g (1oz) sliced pepperoni
2 small mushrooms
25g (1oz) peeled prawns
a small tin of sweetcorn
125g (4oz) grated mozzarella cheese

Heat your oven to 220°C, 425°F, Gas mark 7.

Cut the dough in half, then in half again.

1. Follow the steps on pages 78-79 to make the dough for the bases. When the dough has risen turn on your oven.

2. Put the dough on a floury work surface. Cut it into four and roll each piece into a 15cm (6in) circle. Pinch up the edges.

3. Grease a baking sheet and put the dough circles onto it. Put a tablespoon of milk in a cup and brush each circle with the milk.

4. Cut the ham into small squares. Put these onto one of the bases. Chop up the pineapple ring and lay the pieces on the ham.

5. Slice the tomato finely. Lay them on another base. Cut the basil into small strips and sprinkle them on top.

Try different combinations of ingredients, such as tomato, prawn and mushroom.

6. Lay the slices of pepperoni on the third base. Slice the mushrooms finely and spread them on top of the pepperoni.

7. Open the tin of sweetcorn and drain it. Spread a tablespoon of sweetcorn over the base. Put the prawns on top.

8. Sprinkle each of the pizzas with cheese. Bake them for 15-20 minutes until the bases and cheese are golden brown.

Chicago pizza pie

Makes one 23cm (9in) deep pan pizza

For the dough: 50g (2oz) strong white flour
125g (4oz) plain flour
1 teaspoon of salt
15g (½oz) fresh yeast,
    or 1 teaspoon of easy blend yeast
200ml (7fl oz) warm water
  1 tablespoon of oil

For the tomato sauce: half a tablespoon of olive oil
  half an onion, finely chopped
  1 clove of garlic
  225g (8oz) can of chopped tomatoes
  1 teaspoon of chopped basil
  salt and ground pepper

For the topping: 1 green pepper
  50g (2oz) button mushrooms
  50g (2oz) sliced pepperoni
  175g (6oz) grated mozzarella cheese

a 23/25cm (9/10in) deep pizza tin or sandwich tin

Heat your oven to 220°C, 425°F, Gas mark 7.

1. Follow steps 1-8 on pages 78-79 to make the dough. At step 2, sift both types of flour into the bowl.

2. Put a little oil onto a paper towel and rub over the base and inside of the tin so that they are covered with oil.

3. Sprinkle a little flour onto your work surface and on your rolling pin. Roll the dough into a circle about the size of your tin.

4. Place the dough in the middle of the tin and press it out to the edges with your knuckles. Make it as even as you can.

5. Cover the tin with plastic foodwrap and leave it in a warm place for 20 minutes. It will rise a little bit more.

6. Turn on your oven. While the dough is rising, follow steps 2 to 5 on page 81 to make the tomato sauce.

See the tip on page 89 for cutting peppers.

7. Cut the ends off the pepper. Chop it in half and cut out the seeds. Cut it into cubes. Slice the mushrooms thinly.

8. Spread the sauce over the dough. Lay the pepperoni, then the mushrooms and finally the green pepper, on top.

9. Sprinkle it with grated cheese and bake it for about 20 minutes until the dough is golden and has risen.

Prawn pizza

Makes one 25cm (10in) round pizza

One traditional pizza base - see pages 78-79

For the tomato sauce: 1 tablespoon of olive oil
1 onion
1 clove of garlic
1 level tablespoon of tomato purée
400g (14oz) can of chopped tomatoes
2 teaspoons sugar
1 tablespoon of chopped fresh basil
salt and freshly ground pepper

For the topping: half a red pepper
half a yellow or green pepper
150g (6oz) peeled prawns, thawed, if
    they have been frozen
1 level tablespoon of chopped parsley
1 tablespoon of olive oil

Heat your oven to 220°C, 425°F,
Gas mark 7.

Sprinkle flour on your work surface.

Pinch up a rim around the edge.

1. Follow pages 78-79 to make a pizza base. While the dough is rising, make a tomato sauce following steps 2 to 5 on page 81.

2. When your dough has risen and you have kneaded it again, roll the dough into a 25cm (10in) circle. Turn on your oven.

3. Dip a paper towel in margarine and rub it over a baking sheet to grease it. Lay the dough in the middle of the sheet.

4. Cut the seedy part out of the peppers. Slice them lengthways into strips. Try to cut them as finely as you can (see right).

5. Spread the tomato sauce over the base. Scatter the strips of pepper all over it. Sprinkle it with parsley.

6. If your prawns were frozen, put them into a sieve to drain away any liquid, then scatter them over the top.

You can buy lots of different colours of peppers. It doesn't matter which one you choose for this pizza.

Slicing peppers

7. Sprinkle on some salt and a little black pepper then carefully drizzle the oil from the spoon all over the top.

8. Put your pizza into the oven and bake it for about 20 minutes until the base is crisp and becomes golden brown.

When you slice a pepper, cut it in half then cut out the seeds. Slice it from the inside. It's easier than trying to pierce the skin.

Tomato and courgette pizza

Makes one rectangular pizza 30 x 25cm (14 x 10in)

One scone pizza base (see page 82)

For the topping: 1 tablespoon of olive oil
1 onion
2 cloves of garlic
3 beef tomatoes
1 tablespoon of fresh chopped basil
2 tablespoons of pine nuts
1 small courgette
salt and ground black pepper
150g (6oz) grated mozzarella cheese

Heat your oven to 200°C, 400°F,
Gas mark 6.

1. Turn on your oven before you make the dough. Follow steps 1-3 on page 82 to make a scone dough pizza base.

2. Put the dough onto a floured surface and roll and stretch it into a rectangle about 35 x 28cm (14 x 11in).

3. Grease your baking sheet with margarine and carefully lift the dough onto it. Pinch up the edge all the way around.

4. Peel the onion and slice it into thin rings. Crush the garlic. Gently heat the oil and cook the onion and garlic for three minutes.

5. Spread the onion rings and garlic over the dough. Cut the tomatoes in half and slice them as thinly as you can.

6. Lay the tomatoes on the base, overlapping them a little. Scatter the pine nuts and chopped basil over the top.

7. Trim the ends off the courgette. Hold it in one hand and run a potato peeler along to cut really thin slices.

8. Scatter the courgette slices over the pizza. Season it with a little salt and pepper. Sprinkle on the grated cheese.

9. Put the pizza into the oven and bake for 15-20 minutes until the cheese is golden and bubbling. Serve immediately.

Calzones (folded pizzas)

Makes eight calzones

One traditional pizza base (see pages 78-79)

For the filling: 250g (8oz) ricotta cheese
75g (3oz) smoked ham
100g (4oz) mozzarella cheese
3 large tomatoes
salt and ground black pepper
olive oil

Heat your oven to 220°C, 450°F, Gas mark 7.

1. Follow the steps on pages 78-79 to make traditional dough. While it is rising, chop up the ingredients for the filling.

2. Cut the ham into small pieces. Cut the tomatoes and the mozzarella into small chunks. Turn on your oven.

3. Put both types of cheese, the tomatoes, ham and a pinch of salt and pepper into a bowl. Mix them together well.

Trim the edge to make a circle if you need to.

4. When the dough has risen and you have kneaded it a second time, cut it into eight pieces. Roll the pieces into balls.

5. Sprinkle flour onto a work surface and roll out one of the balls to make a circle about 18cm (7in) across.

6. Put a heaped tablespoon of the mixture onto one half of the circle. Brush a little water around the edge.

7. Fold the dough over the mixture and pinch along the edges to seal the two halves. Make seven more like this.

8. Grease a baking tray with margarine. Lift the calzones onto the tray. Brush them with olive oil and put them in the oven.

9. Bake the calzones for about 20-30 minutes until they have puffed up and have become golden brown.

You can eat the calzones when they are hot or cold.

Patterned edges

Instead of pinching the dough together, you can press a fork around the edge. This leaves a pattern once the calzone is cooked.

Hot apple pizza

Makes one 25cm (10in) round pizza

For the base: 175g (6oz) strong white flour
25g (1oz) butter or margarine
1 teaspoon of easy blend yeast
4 tablespoons of apple juice

For the topping: 2 medium cooking apples
3 tablespoons of apple juice
50g (2oz) raisins
half a teaspoon of cinnamon
1 tablespoon of sugar
3 eating apples
2 tablespoons of lemon juice
1 heaped tablespoon of brown sugar

Heat your oven to 200°C, 400°F, Gas mark 6.

Rub in with your fingers.

1. Sift the flour into a bowl and add the butter or margarine. Rub the butter into the flour until it looks like breadcrumbs.

2. Put the apple juice into a pan and heat it a little to make it warm. Add it, and the yeast to the bowl and stir them well.

3. Continue to stir until you get a soft dough which doesn't stick to the sides of the bowl. Then squeeze it to make a ball.

Lay the circle of dough onto your baking sheet.

4. Sprinkle flour onto a clean, dry work surface. Knead the dough until it is smooth and stretchy (see page 79).

5. Grease a baking sheet with margarine. Rub some flour onto a rolling pin and roll the dough into a 25cm (10in) circle.

6. Pinch up the edge of the dough to make a rim, then cover it with plastic foodwrap. Put it in a warm place for 30 minutes.

7. Peel the cooking apples and cut them in quarters. Cut out the core and then slice the rest of the apple as finely as you can.

8. Put the sliced apple into a small pan. Add the apple juice and cook them with a lid on for 15 minutes until the apple is very soft.

9. Take the pan off the heat and stir the apple to make a smooth sauce, or purée. Add the raisins, sugar and cinnamon.

Cut out the apple cores.

10. Turn the oven on. Peel the eating apples and quarter them. Slice them finely and sprinkle the slices with lemon juice.

11. Spread the purée over the dough with a spoon. Arrange the slices of apple on top, overlapping them a little.

12. Sprinkle the pizza with the brown sugar. Put it into your oven for about 15 minutes or until the dough is golden.

Pasta shapes

Each of the pasta recipes suggests a type or shape of pasta to use. However, if you don't have the right kind, here are a few suggestions for alternative types of pasta you can use. There's also a reminder of names of different types of pasta.

pages 54-55
If you don't have spaghetti, you can use linguine, vermicelli or capelli d'angelo.

page 56
Instead of using fusilli, you can use conchiglie, farfalle or penne.

page 57
If you don't have conchiglie, you can use farfalle, penne or fusilli.

pages 58-59
Use penne instead of macaroni.

page 60-61
Instead of using penne to make this dish you could use conchiglie, farfalle or fusilli.

pages 62-63
If you can't get tagliarini, you can use linguine, spaghetti or fettuccine for this recipe.

page 64
If you don't have ravioli, you can use any filled pasta, such as tortelloni or tortellini.

page 65
If you don't have tortellini, use ravioli or tortelloni, which are the same shape as tortellini, but larger.

pages 66-67
If you can't get conchiglie giganti, use cannelloni (large tubes) instead. Use a teaspoon to fill them with the spinach and ricotta mixture. Turn the cannelloni several times while they are cooking.

page 68-69
You can use fettuccine or tagliarini, instead of tagliatelle.

pages 70-71
You can use tagliatelle instead of egg noodles for this recipe.

page 72-73
You can use any tiny pasta shapes for this recipe. You can also use spaghetti, broken into small pieces. Some supermarkets sell 'soup pasta' which is a mixture of different shapes.

page 74-75
If you don't have vermicelli, you can use spaghetti or capelli d'angelo instead.

page 76-77
If you haven't farfalle, you can use conchiglie, fusilli or penne instead.

Different types of pasta

capelli d'angelo - a very thin type of spaghetti
conchiglie - shells
conchiglie giganti - very large shells.
egg noodles - very thin, flat strands, which are usually dried
farfalle - bows or 'butterflies'
fettuccine - narrow, flat strands
fusilli - spirals
linguine - flat, thin strands
macaroni - small straight or curved tubes
penne - small quill-shaped tubes cut diagonally at both ends
ravioli - square-shaped pasta, which is usually filled with meat, but is sometimes filled with cheese or vegetables.
spaghetti - long, thin, round strands
tagliarini - very thin, flat strands
tagliatelle - flat strands of pasta
tortellini - small, ring-shaped, filled pasta
vermicelli - thin, round strands, thinner than spaghetti

VEGETARIAN
COOKING
FOR BEGINNERS

Vegetarian cooking

All the recipes in this part of the book are vegetarian, which means that they contain no meat or fish. Some of the recipes are suitable for vegans or 'strict vegetarians'. These recipes don't use any animal products at all, including cheese or eggs. They are marked with a (v)* beside the page number in the index (see page 192).

Preparing vegetables

You should wash most fresh vegetables before you prepare them. If you are using mushrooms, don't wash them, but wipe them on a damp paper towel before slicing them. Leeks need to be washed very well to get rid of any soil which is trapped inside. Step 1 on page 122 shows you the easiest way of doing this.

Wash leeks well before you use them.

If you're not sure how to prepare garlic, turn to page 5 where there are steps which show you what to do. On page 55 you can find out how to crush a clove of garlic if you don't have a garlic crusher.

The sections at the top of broccoli or cauliflower are called florets. Cut these off the thick stalk (see page 125).

A clove of garlic is one part of a whole garlic bulb.

Use kitchen scissors to cut up fresh herbs, such as parsley or chives.

Peel carrots and potatoes if they are dirty or big. Wash or scrape new potatoes and small carrots.

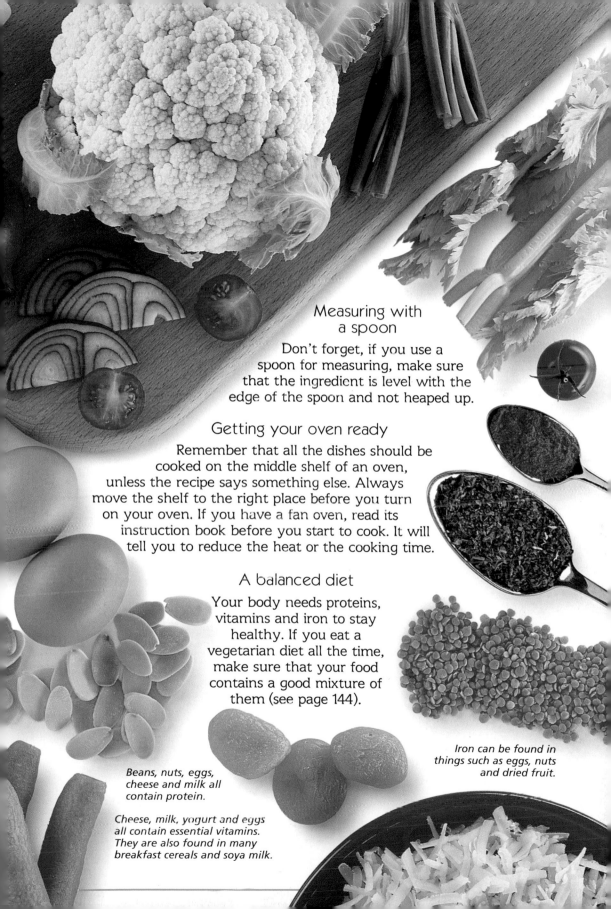

Measuring with a spoon

Don't forget, if you use a spoon for measuring, make sure that the ingredient is level with the edge of the spoon and not heaped up.

Getting your oven ready

Remember that all the dishes should be cooked on the middle shelf of an oven, unless the recipe says something else. Always move the shelf to the right place before you turn on your oven. If you have a fan oven, read its instruction book before you start to cook. It will tell you to reduce the heat or the cooking time.

A balanced diet

Your body needs proteins, vitamins and iron to stay healthy. If you eat a vegetarian diet all the time, make sure that your food contains a good mixture of them (see page 144).

Iron can be found in things such as eggs, nuts and dried fruit.

Beans, nuts, eggs, cheese and milk all contain protein.

Cheese, milk, yogurt and eggs all contain essential vitamins. They are also found in many breakfast cereals and soya milk.

Hints and tips

This page shows you some of the cooking skills which are used in the vegetarian recipes.

Grating cheese

Cut a piece of cheese which weighs more than you need. Grate some, then weigh the grated cheese. Grate more if you need to.

Adding salt and pepper

Try adding a pinch of salt or ground black pepper.

Some recipes tell you to add a little salt and pepper. The amount you add of each depends on your own taste.

Cutting peppers

Use a serrated knife to cut both ends off. Cut the pepper in half from end to end and cut out the part with the seeds.

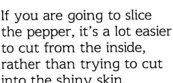

If you are going to slice the pepper, it's a lot easier to cut from the inside, rather than trying to cut into the shiny skin.

Slicing tomatoes

A small serrated knife is best to use to slice a tomato. Cut the tomato in half, then lay its flat-side down and slice it.

Making breadcrumbs

1. Use bread which is two or three days old to make breadcrumbs. Cut off the crusts and tear the slices of bread into pieces.

2. Put the bread into a food processor. Put on the lid and turn it on. Whizz the bread until you get fine crumbs.

Use the small or medium holes on your grater.

If you don't have a food processor, grate stale bread on a cheese grater to make crumbs. Take care, so you don't grate your fingers.

Cheese crunchies

Makes 10-12

50g (2oz) mature Cheddar cheese
100g (4oz) soft 'tub' margarine
50g (2oz) ground rice
50g (2oz) self-raising flour
50g (2oz) plain wholemeal flour
quarter of a teaspoon of salt

Heat your oven to 190°C, 375°F, Gas mark 5.

1. Grate the cheese on the medium holes on your grater. Put the cheese into a large bowl. Add the margarine and ground rice.

2. Shake the flour and the salt through a sieve into the bowl. Add any bits left in the bottom of the sieve.

Use a wooden spoon.

3. Stir everything well until all the ingredients are mixed together. Then, squeeze the mixture into a ball.

4. Sprinkle a clean, dry work surface with a little flour. Put the mixture onto it and shape it into a roll, about 15cm (6in) long.

5. Lay the roll on some plastic foodwrap. Wrap it around the roll. Put the roll into a fridge for about an hour, to chill.

The margarine greases the baking sheets.

6. While the roll is in the fridge, dip a paper towel in some margarine, then rub it over two baking sheets. Turn on your oven.

7. Unwrap the roll and cut it into 1cm (½in) slices. Space out the slices on the baking sheets. They may spread as they cook.

8. Bake them for about 15 minutes until they are golden. When they are cooked, lift them onto a wire rack to cool.

Three-bean dip

Enough for 4-6

400g (14oz) can of butter beans
400g (14oz) pinto beans
400g (14oz) cannellini beans
1 large lemon
1 clove of garlic
4 tablespoons of tahini paste
4 tablespoons of boiling water
2 tablespoons of chopped parsley
salt and ground black pepper

Serve the dip with home-made breadsticks (see opposite), or with crackers.

1. Empty the beans into a sieve or colander. Rinse the beans under cold running water, then drain them. Tip them into a large bowl.

Stir the beans too, to lift those at the bottom.

2. Mash the beans with a fork to make a smoothish mixture. It's quite hard work to begin with. Put a kettle on to boil.

3. Cut the lemon in half. Press and twist each half on a lemon squeezer. Pour the juice into the beans and mash the mixture again.

To serve, spoon the dip into a clean bowl and sprinkle on some more parsley.

4. Peel the garlic clove and crush it. Add the garlic to the beans along with the tahini, boiling water and the parsley.

5. Stir in a little salt and pepper. Then, beat the mixture with a wooden spoon until everything is mixed in thoroughly.

6. Taste it and add more salt and pepper if you need to. Put the dip into a fridge for at least half an hour to chill, then serve.

Breadsticks

Makes about 20

280g (10oz) packet of white or brown bread mix
1 tablespoon of poppy seeds
2 tablespoons of sesame seeds
plain or self-raising flour for sprinkling
margarine for greasing

Heat your oven to 200°C, 400°F, Gas mark 6.

1. Grease two baking sheets with margarine on a paper towel. Open the bread mix and put it in a large bowl.

Find out how to knead dough on page 79.

The dough will become smooth and stretchy.

2. Add the poppy seeds and a tablespoon of sesame seeds. Begin to make the dough, following the instructions on the packet.

3. The instructions will tell you to 'knead' the dough. Put the dough on a floured work surface, then push the dough away from you.

4. Fold the dough in half, turn it and push it away again. Do this for about five minutes. Leave the dough in a bowl to rise.

Cover the rest of the dough in foodwrap while you are rolling each stick.

5. Turn on your oven. Cut the dough in quarters, then cut each quarter into five pieces. Roll each piece into a 20cm (8in) stick.

6. Brush each stick with cold water and sprinkle on the remaining sesame seeds. Space the sticks out on the baking sheets.

7. Cook the breadsticks for 15 minutes, until they turn golden. Use a spatula and fork to lift them onto a wire rack to cool.

Bread and cheese pudding

Enough for 4

margarine for greasing
175g (6oz) stale white bread
100g (4oz) Cheddar cheese
3 eggs
450ml (¾ pint) milk
half a teaspoon of smooth mustard
salt and ground black pepper

quarter of a teaspoon of ground paprika
2 medium tomatoes

a shallow ovenproof dish,
    about 22 x 30cm (8½ x 12in)

Heat your oven to 200°C, 400°F,
Gas mark 6.

1. Dip a paper towel into some margarine. Rub the paper towel over the inside of an ovenproof dish, to grease it.

2. If the bread is unsliced, slice it. Cut the slices into squares, about 2.5cm (1in), leaving the crust on. Put the bread into the dish.

3. Cut the cheese into 1cm (½in) cubes, then scatter them evenly over the bread. Turn your oven on to heat up.

4. Break the eggs into a jug and beat them with a fork. Add the milk, mustard and a little salt and pepper, and whisk it.

5. Slowly pour the milky mixture over the bread and cheese. Make sure that all the pieces are coated with the mixture.

6. Leave the dish to stand for five minutes, so that the egg and milk mixture is absorbed into the bread and it goes slightly soggy.

7. Sprinkle small pinches of paprika over the top. Wash your hands after touching it because it will sting if you accidently rub your eyes.

Use a serrated knife.

8. Cut the tomatoes in half and slice them as thinly as you can. Lay the slices in rows on top of the bread and cheese.

9. Put the dish into the oven and bake it for 35 minutes, until the bread is golden brown and the cheese is bubbling.

Tropical spiced rice

Enough for 4

25g (1oz) creamed coconut
225g (8oz) can of pineapple pieces in natural juice
quarter of a teaspoon of ground tumeric
salt and ground white pepper
225g (8oz) basmati and wild rice
8 spring onions
1 tablespoon of sunflower oil
quarter of a teaspoon of ground coriander
50g (2oz) frozen peas, thawed
25g (1oz) sultanas

You could use long grain rice for this recipe. Follow the cooking instructions on its packet.

1. Put a kettle of water on to boil. Cut the creamed coconut into small pieces and put them in a measuring jug.

2. Pour 600ml (1 pint) of boiling water into the jug. Stir the mixture well until all the pieces of coconut have dissolved.

3. Drain the pieces of pineapple through a sieve or colander into a large jug or bowl. Don't throw away the pineapple juice.

Don't lift the lid while it cooks.

4. Pour the coconut liquid and the pineapple juice into a large pan. Add the tumeric and half a teaspoon of salt. Bring it to the boil.

5. Put the rice into a sieve and rinse it well under cold water. Add the rice to the pan and bring it back to the boil.

6. Turn the heat down so that the water is just bubbling. Put a lid on the pan. Cook the rice gently for 20 minutes.

7. While the rice is cooking, cut the top and bottom off the spring onions. Slice the onions into 2.5cm (1in) pieces.

8. Heat the oil in a frying pan over a medium heat. Add the onions and cook them for four minutes, stirring occasionally.

Cooking rice

9. Sprinkle the coriander over the onions and cook for one minute, stirring all the time. Then, turn the heat off under this pan.

Stir it all the time.

10. When the rice is cooked, add the pineapple, peas, onions, sultanas and some pepper. Cook it for a minute, then eat it while it's hot.

If rice sticks together when it is cooked, separate the grains by stirring lightly with a fork.

Italian bread

Enough for 4

450g (1lb) strong plain white flour
1 level teaspoon of easy-blend
   dried yeast
300ml (½ pint) warm water

flour for sprinkling
margarine for greasing
6 tablespoons of olive oil
1 teaspoon of sea salt

a baking sheet, greased with margarine

1. Shake the flour through a sieve into a large bowl. Stir in the easy-blend yeast, then make a hollow in the middle of the flour.

2. Pour the warm water into the hollow, along with five tablespoons of oil. Mix it into the flour with a wooden spoon.

3. Carry on mixing until you get a soft dough which doesn't stick to the sides of the bowl. Then, wash your hands.

Sprinkle about two tablespoons of flour on your work surface.

4. Sprinkle flour onto a clean, dry work surface. Dip a paper towel in margarine and grease inside a large bowl.

5. Wash your hands well. 'Knead' the dough for about five minutes (see page 79), then put it into the greased bowl.

6. Cover the bowl with plastic foodwrap. Leave it in a warm place for an hour, until the dough rises to twice its size.

Remember to grease the baking sheet first.

7. Then, knead the dough again for a couple of minutes, to burst all the large air bubbles which have formed inside it.

8. Sprinkle some flour onto a rolling pin, then roll out the dough to make a circle about 25cm (10in) across.

9. Put the dough on a baking sheet. Rub oil onto a piece of foodwrap and cover the bread. Turn your oven on to 220°C, 425°F, Gas mark 7.

Dip your finger in flour before you press it in.

10. Leave the baking sheet in a warm place (not in the oven!) for 20 minutes. Take off the foodwrap. Make dimples all over the top.

11. Brush the top with a tablespoon of oil, then sprinkle the sea salt over the top. Put the baking sheet into the oven.

12. Bake the bread for 25 minutes, until it is golden. Leave it on a wire rack to cool. Cut it into wedges, then add a filling you like.

Mexican bean soup

Enough for 4

1 small red onion
1 clove of garlic
1 tablespoon of olive oil
200g (7oz) can of red kidney beans
half a teaspoon of mild chilli powder
400g (14oz) can of chopped
tomatoes with herbs
1 vegetable stock cube

1. Peel the skin off the onion and chop the onion finely. Peel the clove of garlic and crush it. Put a kettle on to boil.

2. Heat the oil in a large saucepan over a medium heat. Cook the onion and garlic for about five minutes until they are soft.

3. Open the can of beans, then pour them into a sieve or colander to drain them. Rinse the beans under the cold tap.

Stir until the stock cube dissolves.

4. Add the beans to the pan, along with the chilli powder and chopped tomatoes. Stir everything together well.

5. Crumble the stock cube into a measuring jug. Pour in 150ml (¼ pint) of boiling water and stir well. Pour the stock into the pan.

6. Turn up the heat so that the mixture boils. Then, when it is boiling, turn the heat down so that the soup bubbles gently.

Softening onions

7. Put a lid on the pan and let the soup bubble for about ten minutes. Stir it occasionally to stop it from sticking.

8. Take the pan off the heat. Ladle the soup into bowls. Don't try to pour it out as it may splash. Eat it while it's hot.

When you soften onions, let them sizzle gently in oil, stirring occasionally. Turn the heat down if the onion begins to go brown.

Cracked wheat risotto

Enough for 4

4 spring onions
100g (4oz) button mushrooms
3 tablespoons of sunflower oil
50g (2oz) flaked almonds
1 vegetable stock cube
225g (8oz) cracked wheat
8 ready-to-eat dried apricots
4 sprigs of fresh parsley
salt and ground black pepper

Stir the almonds all the time, as they burn easily.

1. Cut the tops and bottoms off the spring onions. Cut the onions diagonally into pieces, about 2.5cm (1in) long.

2. Wipe the mushrooms with a damp paper towel to clean them. Then, slice each mushroom thinly. Put a kettle on to boil.

3. Put about half a tablespoon of oil into a saucepan, over a medium heat. Cook the almonds until they are golden.

A slotted spoon has holes in it.

Stir until the cube dissolves.

4. Put a paper towel onto a plate. Use a slotted spoon to lift the almonds onto it. Then, heat the remaining oil in the pan.

5. Add the mushrooms and spring onions to the pan. Cook them gently for five minutes, until they are soft. Stir them often.

6. Meanwhile, crumble the stock cube into a measuring jug. Pour in 600ml (1 pint) of boiling water and stir.

Take off the lid and stir it occasionally.

7. Add the cracked wheat to the pan and stir it for a minute. Pour in the stock, then turn the heat up so that the mixture boils.

8. Once it has boiled, turn the heat down and put a lid on the pan. Let the mixture bubble gently for about ten minutes.

9. Use kitchen scissors to snip the apricots into small pieces. Add the pieces to the bubbling mixture, along with some salt and pepper.

Use kitchen scissors.

10. Take the lid off the pan. Let the mixture cook for five minutes more, or until all the stock has been absorbed.

11. While the mixture is cooking, break the stalks off the parsley. Put the leaves into a mug and snip them into small pieces.

12. Stir the parsley and half of the flaked almonds into the mixture. Sprinkle the rest of the almonds on top and serve immediately.

Soya bolognese sauce

Enough for 4

1 onion
1 stick of celery
100g (4oz) button mushrooms
2 medium carrots
1 clove of garlic
3 tablespoons of olive oil
1 vegetable stock cube

400g (14oz) can of chopped tomatoes
1 teaspoon of dried mixed herbs
75g (3oz) soya mince
salt and ground black pepper
375g (12oz) dried pasta or 450g (15oz)
    fresh pasta
15g (½oz) margarine

1. Cut the ends off the onion and celery. Peel the onion and wash the celery. Cut both the onion and celery into thin slices.

2. Wipe the mushrooms with a damp paper towel. Cut them into thick slices. Peel or scrape the carrots, then slice them finely.

3. Peel and crush the garlic. Heat two tablespoons of oil in a large pan over a low heat. Add the onion and cook it for three minutes.

4. Add the celery, carrots, mushrooms and garlic. Cook them for five minutes, until the onion begins to turn brown.

5. While the vegetables are cooking, put a kettle on to boil. Crumble the stock cube into a measuring jug.

6. Pour 600ml (1 pint) of boiling water into the measuring jug and stir until the stock cube dissolves.

Stir it occasionally to stop it from sticking.

7. Pour the stock into the pan. Add the chopped tomatoes, dried herbs and a little salt and pepper. Stir the mixture well.

8. Stir in the soya mince. Turn up the heat and bring the mixture to the boil. Then, turn down the heat so that it bubbles gently.

9. Put a lid on the pan and cook the mixture for 30 minutes. The mixture will thicken as the mince soaks up the stock.

The oil will stop the pasta from sticking.

Drain the pasta in a colander.

10. About 15 minutes before the sauce is ready, half-fill a large pan with water. Add a tablespoon of oil and a pinch of salt.

11. Bring the water to the boil and add the pasta. Look at the instructions on the packet of pasta and cook it for the time it says.

12. When the pasta is cooked, drain it, then put it back into the pan. Add the margarine and shake the pan to coat the pasta.

13. Put the pasta onto four plates or bowls. Ladle some sauce on top and eat it immediately.

Cheese and tomato tart

Enough for 4-6

375g (13oz) packet of ready-rolled puff pastry
1 tablespoon of milk
1 large onion
1 medium courgette
3 tablespoons of olive oil
half a teaspoon of dried oregano
salt and ground black pepper
225g (8oz) cherry tomatoes
225g (8oz) mozzarella cheese

Trim the pastry to fit the tray.

1. Turn on your oven to 220°C, 425°F, Gas mark 7. Unroll the pastry. Put it on a baking sheet. Trim one end off, if you need to.

The onion and courgette will soften.

2. Put the milk into a cup. Use a pastry brush to brush the milk around the edge of the pastry, to make a 1cm (½in) border.

3. Cut the ends off the onion and peel it. Cut it finely. Cut the ends off the courgette and cut it into 1cm (½in) slices.

4. Heat the oil over a lowish heat and add the onion. Cook it for five minutes. Add the courgette and cook for five minutes more.

5. Stir in the oregano and add some salt and pepper. Spoon the mixture over the pastry, but do not cover the milky border.

6. Use a serrated knife to cut the tomatoes in half. Arrange the tomatoes on top of the mixture, with their cut-side upwards.

This tart is delicious served hot or warm.

7. Open the bag of cheese and pour away any liquid. Cut the cheese into 1cm (½in) cubes. Scatter them evenly over the tomatoes.

8. Put the tart on the middle shelf of the oven for 35-40 minutes, until the pastry rises around the edges and turns brown.

9. Leave the tart on the baking sheet for three minutes. Cut the tart into eight pieces. Use a fish slice to lift each piece.

Veggie burgers

Makes 8

1 onion
1 stick of celery
1 red pepper
2 tablespoons of sunflower oil
1 clove of garlic
175g (6oz) dried red lentils
1 vegetable stock cube
half a teaspoon of yeast extract
75g (3oz) fresh breadcrumbs
50g (2oz) chopped nuts
ground black pepper

Stir it occasionally.

1. Cut the ends off the onion and celery. Peel the onion and wash the celery. Cut them both into very thin pieces.

2. Slice the ends off the red pepper. Cut it in half and cut out the seeds. Cut each half into thin strips. Cut the strips into cubes.

3. Put a kettle on to boil. Heat the oil in a saucepan over a medium heat. Cook the onion and celery for five minutes, until soft.

Stir it all the time, to coat everything with oil.

4. Peel and crush the garlic. Add it to the pan, along with the red pepper and lentils. Cook them for about a minute.

5. Crumble the stock cube into a measuring jug and pour in 350ml (12floz) of boiling water. Add the yeast extract and stir well.

6. Pour the stock into the pan and bring it to the boil. Then, turn the heat down until the mixture bubbles gently. Put a lid on the pan.

Cover it with plastic foodwrap.

7. Cook the mixture for 25 minutes, or until the lentils have absorbed all the stock. Spoon the mixture into a large bowl.

8. Mix in the breadcrumbs, nuts and some pepper. Let the mixture cool, then cover it. Put it in a fridge for at least 30 minutes.

9. When chilled, divide the mixture into eight pieces. Sprinkle some flour on a chopping board and roll each piece into a ball.

Use a fish slice
to turn the
burgers over.

10. Turn your grill on to medium. Press each ball into a burger shape and brush the top of each one with a little oil.

11. Put the burgers onto the grill-pan rack. Cook them under the grill for five minutes, until they are slightly browned.

12. Turn the burgers over. Brush the tops with a little more oil and cook them for five more minutes. Eat them while they are hot.

Mushroom croustade

Enough for 4

For the case:
25g (1oz) plain wholemeal flour
50g (2oz) porridge oats
100g (4oz) wholemeal breadcrumbs
 (find out how to make breadcrumbs
 on page 100)
100g (4oz) butter or margarine

For the filling:
225g (8oz) button mushrooms
1 tablespoon of sunflower oil
2 eggs
150g (5oz) full-fat soft vegetarian
 cheese with herbs and garlic
salt and ground black pepper

a 20cm (8in) flan dish

Mix them with a wooden spoon.

1. Turn your oven on to 200°C, 400°F, Gas mark 6. For the case, put the flour, porridge oats and breadcrumbs into a bowl.

2. Gently melt the butter or margarine in a pan over a low heat. Pour in the mixture from the bowl and mix it well.

3. Spoon the mixture into a flan dish. Use the back of a spoon to press it firmly onto the bottom and up the sides of the dish.

The baking sheet helps the mixture to cook on the bottom.

4. Put the dish onto a baking sheet. Bake it on the middle shelf of your oven for ten minutes. Take it out of the oven.

5. Turn the oven down to 180°C, 350°F, Gas mark 4. Wipe the mushrooms using a damp paper towel, then cut them in half.

Stir the mushrooms occasionally.

6. Heat the oil in a frying pan over a low heat. Add the mushrooms and cook them for five minutes, until they are soft.

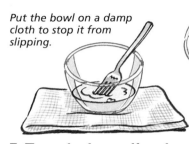

Put the bowl on a damp cloth to stop it from slipping.

7. Turn the heat off under the mushrooms. Break the eggs into a small bowl and beat them with a fork until they are mixed.

Use a wooden spoon.

8. Put the cheese into a bowl and stir it. Add the beaten egg, a little at a time. Stir the mixture each time you add some egg.

9. Add the mushrooms to the mixture, but don't add any of the juice left in the pan. Add some salt and pepper and stir well.

The croustade is delicious served with a salad or green vegetables.

10. Spoon the mixture into the case and smooth the top with the back of a spoon. Press in any mushrooms sticking up.

11. Put the dish into the oven for 25 minutes and bake it until the filling has set and the crust is golden. Serve it hot or cold.

Cheesy sausages

Makes 8

1 small leek
15g (½oz) butter
100g (4oz) Cheddar cheese
8 fresh chives
2 eggs
salt and ground black pepper
quarter of a teaspoon of smooth mustard
175g (6oz) white breadcrumbs
plain flour for sprinkling
2 tablespoons of sunflower oil

Slice half way along the leek from the green end, like this.

Use a small saucepan.

Snip the chives over the bowl.

1. Cut the roots and green tops off the leek. Make a slice half way along the leek and rinse it really well to get rid of any soil. Then, slice the leek finely.

2. Melt the butter in a saucepan over a medium heat. Add the slices of leek and cook gently for about five minutes, until soft. Don't let them go brown.

3. Spoon the leek into a big bowl. Grate the cheese finely and add it to the bowl. Use kitchen scissors to snip the chives into small pieces and add them too.

Put a damp dishcloth under the bowl to stop it from slipping as you beat.

Find out how to make breadcrumbs on page 100.

4. Break the eggs into a small bowl. Add some salt and pepper and the mustard. Beat them lightly until the yolks, egg white and mustard are mixed.

5. Pour the beaten egg mixture into the big bowl and add the breadcrumbs. Stir everything together with a wooden spoon until it is mixed well.

6. Sprinkle a little flour onto a clean, dry work surface. Put the mixture onto the flour and cut it into eight equal pieces with a knife.

Turn the sausages often as they cook.

7. Wash your hands and dry them. Rub a little flour on your hands, then roll each piece into the shape of a sausage. Put the sausages onto a plate.

8. Cover the sausages with some plastic foodwrap. Put the plate into a fridge for about 20 minutes, to make the sausages really firm.

9. When the sausages are ready, heat the oil in a frying pan over a medium heat. Add the sausages and cook them for ten minutes. Serve immediately.

Chunky vegetable goulash

Enough for 4

1 onion
1 clove of garlic
2 carrots
2 medium-sized potatoes

half a medium-sized cauliflower
1 tablespoon of vegetable oil
3 teaspoons of paprika
2 tablespoons of plain flour
1 vegetable stock cube
400g (14oz) can of chopped tomatoes
with basil or mixed herbs
salt and ground black pepper
150ml (¼ pint) soured
cream

1. Cut the top and bottom off the onion. Peel the onion and cut it into small chunks. Peel the clove of garlic and crush it.

2. Peel or scrape the carrots and cut them in half. Cut them lengthways, then slice them into pieces about 2.5cm (1in) long.

3. Peel the potatoes and cut them in half. Cut each piece of potato into 1cm (½in) slices, then cut the slices into cubes.

4. Pull any leaves off the cauliflower and throw them away. Cut the florets off the cauliflower's stalk (see tip below).

5. Heat the oil in a large pan over a lowish heat. Gently cook the onion and garlic for five minutes, until they are soft.

6. While the onions are cooking, put a kettle on to boil. Sprinkle two teaspoons of paprika over the onions. Add the flour and stir well.

7. Crumble the stock cube into a measuring jug and pour in 600ml (1 pint) of boiling water. Stir it until the stock cube dissolves.

8. Pour the stock into the pan. Add the tomatoes, carrots, potatoes and the cauliflower florets, as well as a little salt and pepper.

9. Turn the heat up and bring the mixture to the boil. Then, turn down the heat so that the mixture bubbles gently.

Cutting cauliflower

10. Put a lid onto the pan. Leave everything to bubble gently for about 20-25 minutes, until the vegetables are cooked.

11. Use a ladle to put the goulash into bowls. Spoon on some soured cream and sprinkle the remaining paprika on top.

Cut into the stalk about 1cm (½in) from a floret. Pull the floret out, then cut off another one.

Baked Spanish omelette

Serves 4

margarine for greasing
1 onion
2 medium-sized potatoes
2 tablespoons of olive oil
1 clove of garlic
100g (4oz) frozen peas, thawed
4 eggs
150ml (¼ pint) milk
salt and ground black pepper

a shallow 20cm (8in) ovenproof dish

Stir it occasionally.

1. Turn your oven on to 180°C, 350°F, Gas mark 4. Dip a paper towel in some margarine, then rub it over the inside of the dish.

2. Peel the onion and cut it finely. Peel the potatoes and cut them in half. Cut them into 1cm (½in) slices. Cut the slices into cubes.

3. Heat the oil in a frying pan over a medium heat. Add the onion and potato and cook for four minutes, until they begin to soften.

Stir it all the time.

4. Peel and crush the garlic. Add it to the pan and cook for two minutes more, until the onion and potatoes begin to brown.

5. Take the pan off the heat. Spoon the onion and potato into the bottom of the dish spreading it out evenly. Add the peas too.

6. Break the eggs into a small bowl. Beat them with a fork, then stir in the milk and a little salt and black pepper.

7. Pour the beaten egg over the vegetables in the dish. Bake the omelette in the oven for 45 minutes until it has set.

8. To check that it is cooked, push a knife into the middle of it. If lots of liquid seeps out, cook it for a few more minutes.

9. Run a knife around the edge of the dish to loosen the omelette, then cut it into quarters. Use a spatula or fish slice to serve it.

Other fillings : Cheese

Sprinkle 50g (2oz) of grated Gruyère cheese and one tablespoon of chopped parsley over the vegetables, at step 5.

Mushroom

For a mushroom omelette, leave out the peas. Slice 100g (4oz) of mushrooms. Cook them with the onions and potatoes at step 3.

Tomato

Slice two medium-sized tomatoes as finely as you can. Arrange the slices on top of the cooked vegetables, at step 5.

Sweetcorn

Drain a 200g (7oz) can of sweetcorn in a sieve or colander. Sprinkle the corn over the vegetables at step 5.

Cheese bites with tomato sauce

Enough for 4

For the tomato sauce:
1 red onion
1 tablespoon of olive oil
400g (14oz) can of chopped tomatoes
2 tablespoons of soy sauce
2 teaspoons of red wine vinegar
1 teaspoon of soft brown sugar

For the cheese bites:
75g (3oz) white breadcrumbs
2 tablespoons of plain flour
225g (8oz) Cheddar cheese
salt and ground black pepper
2 eggs (you only need the whites)
oil for frying

Grate the cheese on the medium holes on your grater.

Slice the onion as thinly as you can.

1. Make the breadcrumbs (see page 4). Put 50g (2oz) of the breadcrumbs into a bowl. Grate the cheese, add it to the bowl and stir well.

2. Put the bowl on one side while you make the sauce. Cut the ends off the onion and peel it. Cut it in half, then slice it.

3. Put the olive oil into a pan over a low heat. Cook the slices of onion for five minutes, stirring them occasionally.

4. Add the tomatoes, soy sauce, vinegar and sugar and stir it well. Turn up the heat and bring the mixture to the boil.

5. Once the mixture has boiled, turn down the heat and let it bubble gently. Put a lid on the pan and cook for 15 minutes.

6. Make the bites while the sauce is cooking. Shake the flour and some salt and pepper through a sieve onto the cheese.

Make sure that the bowl is clean before you start.

You don't need the yolks.

7. Carefully break one egg onto a saucer. Put an egg cup over the yolk. Tip the saucer over a bowl so that the white dribbles into it.

8. Do the same with the other egg. Whisk the egg white until it is stiff and makes points or 'peaks' when you lift your whisk.

9. If the tomato sauce is ready while you are still cooking the bites, turn down the heat under it, as low as it will go.

10. Stir a large spoonful of the egg white into the cheese and breadcrumb mixture. Then, gently stir in the rest of the white.

11. Wash your hands. Put the remaining breadcrumbs onto a plate. Make 16 balls with the mixture, about the size of table-tennis balls.

12. Roll the balls in the crumbs to coat them. Pour about 1cm (½in) of oil into a frying pan. Turn the heat on to medium.

Use a spatula to lift them into the pan.

13. After a minute or so, put eight balls into the pan. Cook them for five minutes. Turn the balls as they cook so they are golden all over.

14. Use a slotted spoon to lift them out. Put them onto some kitchen paper to drain. Cook the rest of the balls in the same way.

15. Put four balls onto each plate. Stir the tomato sauce, then spoon it over the balls. Eat them while they are hot.

You could put some sauce onto each plate before you add the bites. Spoon any remaining sauce on top.

Tofu skewers with noodles

Enough for 4

two 285g (10oz) packets of firm tofu
2 tablespoons of soy sauce
1 small onion
1 clove of garlic
2 tablespoons of sunflower oil
25g (1oz) creamed coconut
1 tablespoon of lemon or lime juice

2 teaspoons of soft brown sugar
quarter of a teaspoon of chilli powder
2 tablespoons of crunchy peanut butter

For the noodles:
1 tablespoon of oil
225g (8oz) dried or 350g (12oz) fresh
   egg noodles
1 vegetable stock cube
2 tablespoons of chopped parsley
   or coriander

eight skewers, kebab or saté sticks
   (If you use wooden sticks, soak
      them in water for ten
         minutes before you begin.)

Use a medium heat.

1. Open the packets of tofu and drain off any liquid. Pat the tofu dry on a paper towel, then cut it into 2.5cm (1in) cubes.

2. Push the cubes onto the sticks. Put a tablespoon of soy sauce into a bowl and brush it all over the cubes. Put a kettle on to boil.

3. Peel the onion and cut it finely. Peel and crush the garlic. Heat the oil in a saucepan and cook the onion and garlic until soft.

Stir until the coconut dissolves.

4. Cut the creamed coconut into small pieces and put it into a bowl. Pour in three tablespoons of boiling water and stir.

5. Add the lemon or lime juice, the brown sugar, chilli powder, peanut butter and a tablespoon of soy sauce.

6. Stir everything together until they are blended, then mix in the onion and garlic. Brush the mixture over the tofu.

The oil stops the noodles from sticking together.

Watch the tofu, it can burn easily.

7. Half-fill a large saucepan with water and bring it to the boil. Crumble the stock cube and stir it in. Add a tablespoon of oil.

8. Turn the grill on to a medium heat. Put the tofu sticks onto the rack in the grill pan and put the pan under the grill.

9. Cook the tofu for eight minutes in total. Every two minutes, turn the sticks and brush the tofu with more peanut mixture.

Time the cooking from when the noodles began to boil.

10. Meanwhile, add the noodles to the water. Let the water boil again, then turn down the heat so the water bubbles gently.

11. Cook the noodles for the time it says on their packet, then drain them. Put them back into the pan. Add the parsley or coriander.

12. Toss the noodles in the parsley or coriander. Put the noodles onto plates and lay two tofu sticks on top. Eat them hot.

Baked eggs

Enough for 4

1 medium onion
1 small red pepper
1 small yellow pepper
1 clove of garlic
1 courgette
2 tablespoons of olive oil

400g (14oz) can of chopped tomatoes
1 teaspoon of dried mixed herbs
salt and ground black pepper
butter or margarine for greasing
4 eggs

a shallow, ovenproof dish

1. Turn on your oven to 190°C, 375°F, Gas mark 5. Cut the ends off the onion and peel it. Slice the onion as finely as you can.

2. Slice the ends off the peppers and cut them in half. Cut out the seeds. Cut the peppers into strips, then into cubes.

3. Peel the clove of garlic and crush it in a garlic press. Cut the ends off the courgette and cut it into thin slices.

Stir the mixture occasionally.

4. Heat the oil in a pan over a medium heat. Add the onions, garlic, peppers and courgette. Cook them for ten minutes.

5. When the vegetables are soft, add the tomatoes, dried herbs and a pinch of salt and pepper. Stir it and let the mixture bubble.

6. Leave the mixture to cook for about five minutes or until the sauce becomes thicker and the amount has reduced a little.

7. While the mixture is cooking, dip a paper towel into some margarine or butter. Rub it over an ovenproof dish to grease it.

Space the hollows evenly.

8. When the mixture is ready, spoon it into the dish. Use the back of the spoon to make four hollows in the mixture.

9. Carefully crack an egg into each hollow. Lift the dish into the oven, without letting the eggs spill out over the mixture.

Breaking eggs

Bake the mixture until the egg whites have set.

Bake the mixture until the egg whites have set.

10. Cook the eggs for about 10-15 minutes if you like runny yolks, or 15-20 minutes if you like your eggs well-cooked.

To break an egg, tap it sharply on the side of a bowl or a cup. Tap it again, but harder, if the shell doesn't crack first time.

Push your thumbs inside the crack and pull the shell apart gently. Try not to let any pieces of shell fall into the bowl or cup.

Vegetarian sausages in batter

Enough for 4

275g (10oz) packet of vegetarian sausages,
   thawed if frozen
1 medium courgette
6 cherry tomatoes
50g (2oz) plain flour

quarter of a teaspoon of salt
75ml (3fl oz) milk
1 egg
25g (1oz) solid white vegetable fat

a 20cm (8in) round tin

Use a large bowl.

1. Turn your oven on to 220°C, 425°F, Gas mark 7, to heat up. Cut each sausage into three equal-sized pieces.

2. Cut the ends off the courgette. Cut it into 2.5cm (1in) slices. Prick the skin of each tomato with the tip of a sharp knife.

3. To make the batter, shake the flour and salt through a sieve. Then, make a hollow in the middle of the flour.

4. Pour the milk into a measuring jug and add 75ml (3floz) of cold water to make 150ml (¼ pint) of liquid altogether.

5. Break the egg into a cup, then pour it into the hollow in the flour. Pour in half of the milky liquid from the jug, too.

Whisk it until you get a smooth batter.

6. Mix the milky liquid with the flour. Add the rest of the liquid, a little at a time. Whisk it well each time you add some.

7. Put the fat into the tin and put it in the oven for five minutes. Then, wearing oven gloves, very carefully lift the tin out.

8. Spread the sausages and vegetables around the tin. Take care, the fat will be hot. Then, pour the batter over them.

9. Bake it on the top shelf of the oven for 30-35 minutes, until it has risen and has turned golden. Cut into four and serve.

Tortillas with black bean sauce

Enough for 4

margarine or oil for greasing
1 small onion
1 clove of garlic
1 tablespoon of olive oil
two 400g (14oz) cans of black-eyed
   beans or red kidney beans
two 400g (14oz) cans of chopped
   tomatoes with herbs
1 tablespoon of tomato purée

1 teaspoon of mild chilli powder
salt and ground black pepper
175g (6oz) Gruyère or Cheddar cheese
8 ready-made flour tortillas
150ml (¼ pint) soured cream or thick
   plain yogurt

a large shallow, ovenproof dish, about
   35 x 20cm (14 x 8in)

Heat your oven to 200°C, 400°F,
Gas mark 6.

1. Dip a paper towel into some margarine or pour a little oil onto it. Rub the paper towel inside the dish, to grease it.

2. Turn your oven on. Cut the ends off the onion and peel it, then slice it finely. Peel the clove of garlic and crush it.

3. Heat the oil in a saucepan. Cook the onion and the garlic over a medium heat for five minutes, until soft.

Drain the beans in a sieve or a colander.

4. Drain the beans. Rinse them under cold running water. Add them to the pan and cook for a minute, stirring all the time.

5. Stir in the chopped tomatoes, tomato purée and the chilli powder. Add a little salt and pepper, too.

6. Turn up the heat and bring the sauce to the boil. Then, turn the heat down so that the sauce is still bubbling, but more gently.

The sauce should be thick enough to sit on the spoon.

7. Let the sauce cook for 20 minutes, stirring now and then to stop it from sticking. The sauce should begin to thicken.

8. If your sauce doesn't start to thicken, turn the heat up a little until the mixture bubbles more fiercely. Stir it often.

9. While the sauce is cooking, grate the cheese on the large holes on the grater. Lay the tortillas on a clean, dry work surface.

*Take care as you roll them.
The sauce is still hot.*

10. Divide the sauce between the tortillas. Spread it out almost to the edges, with the back of a spoon.

11. Sprinkle half of the cheese over the tortillas, then roll them up. Then, lay them, join-side down, in the dish.

12. Sprinkle the rest of the cheese over the tortillas. Bake them for 15 minutes, then serve them with the soured cream or yogurt.

Stuffed peppers

Enough for 4

4 medium peppers
4 tablespoons of olive oil
1 vegetable stock cube
175g (6oz) long-grain rice
1 small red onion
1 clove of garlic
200g (7oz) can of chopped tomatoes
half a teaspoon of dried mixed herbs
50g (2oz) frozen peas, thawed
salt and ground black pepper

1. Turn your oven on to 200°C, 400°F, Gas mark 6. Wash and dry the peppers, then put them onto a baking tray.

2. Put two tablespoons of oil in a cup. Brush it over the peppers. Put the tray into the oven and bake the peppers for 12 minutes.

3. When the peppers are cooked, leave them until they are cool enough to touch. Cut them in half from top to bottom.

Pour the stock into a large pan.

4. Cut the stalk, core and seeds from each pepper. Pat the peppers dry, then put them back onto the tray. Put a kettle on to boil.

5. Crumble the stock cube into a jug. Pour 600ml (1 pint) of boiling water into the jug. Stir well and pour the stock into a pan.

6. Add another 600ml (1 pint) of boiling water. Pour in the rice and stir. Turn the heat down so the mixture bubbles gently.

7. Leave the rice to cook for about ten minutes until it is just tender, then drain it in a large sieve over a sink.

8. While the rice is cooking, cut the ends off the onion and peel it. Slice the onion as thinly as you can. Peel and crush the garlic.

9. Heat two tablespoons of oil in a pan. Add the onion and garlic, and cook them gently until they are soft.

The oil stops the foil from sticking to the peppers.

10. Stir in the tomatoes, herbs and a little salt and pepper. Leave the mixture to bubble gently for about five minutes.

11. Add the rice and peas to the tomato mixture and mix everything well. Spoon the mixture into the halves of pepper.

12. Spread a little oil onto the dull side of a piece of foil. Cover the peppers. Put them into the oven for ten minutes. Eat while hot.

Spinach strudel

Enough for 4

50g (2oz) pine nuts
175g (6oz) frozen chopped spinach, thawed
250g (9oz) ricotta cheese
quarter of a teaspoon of grated nutmeg

salt and ground black pepper
40g (1½oz) butter
100g (4oz) filo pastry (about 8 sheets)
1 tablespoon of poppy seeds

Heat your oven to 200°C, 400°F, Gas mark 6.

1. Turn on your oven. Put the pine nuts on a baking sheet. Bake them in the oven for five minutes, until golden. Let them cool.

2. Put the spinach into a sieve. Press the spinach with the back of a large spoon, to squeeze out as much liquid as you can.

3. Tip the spinach into a bowl. Add the pine nuts, the ricotta cheese, nutmeg and a little salt and pepper. Mix everything together.

Cover the rest of the pastry, (see tip, below right).

Don't forget to brush each sheet with butter before putting another one on top.

4. Put the butter into a small saucepan. Heat it very gently over a low heat until the butter melts. Don't let it burn.

5. Carefully lift one sheet of filo pastry and put it on a clean tea towel. Brush the sheet of pastry with some of the melted butter.

6. Put another sheet of filo pastry on top and brush it with butter. Add the other sheets of pastry, one by one, in the same way.

Spread out the mixture with a spatula.

Roll it like a Swiss roll.

7. Spoon the spinach mixture onto the pastry. Spread it over the pastry, leaving a 2.5cm (1in) border around the edge.

8. Fold each of the short sides of pastry over carefully, so that they overlap the edge of the spinach mixture.

9. Fold one of the long sides of pastry over onto the mixture. Then, roll it over and over until you reach the other long side.

10. Brush some of the melted butter over a baking sheet to grease it. Lift the strudel onto it, join-side down.

11. Brush the top and sides of the strudel with the rest of the melted butter. Sprinkle poppy seeds all over the top.

12. Bake the strudel in the oven for 20 minutes, until it is golden and crisp. Cut it into slices and serve straight away.

Using filo pastry

To stop filo pastry from drying out, cover the sheets of pastry with a clean, damp tea towel until you need to use them.

Nut crumble

Enough for 4

1 carrot
1 parsnip
225g (8oz) broccoli
225g (8oz) swede
225g (8oz) celeriac
salt and ground black pepper
1 onion
40g (1½oz) butter
40g (1½oz) plain flour

450ml (¾ pint) milk
margarine for greasing

For the crumble:
100g (4oz) plain flour
50g (2oz) butter
25g (1oz) porridge oats
50g (2oz) chopped mixed nuts

a large ovenproof dish

1. Turn your oven on to 190°C, 375°F, Gas mark 5. Peel the carrot and the parsnip. Cut them into 2.5cm (1in) pieces.

2. Cut the florets off the broccoli stalks. Peel the swede and celeriac and cut them in half. Cut each half into 2.5cm (1in) slices.

3. Cut the slices of swede and celeriac into cubes. Half-fill a large saucepan with water and add half a teaspoon of salt.

4. Bring the pan of water to the boil. Add the carrot, parsnip, swede and celeriac and bring the water back to the boil.

5. Turn down the heat so that the water bubbles gently, then put a lid on the pan. Leave it to cook for five minutes.

6. Add the broccoli and cook it for five minutes more. Ladle 150ml (¼ pint) of the cooking water into a jug. Drain away the rest.

Stir the onion occasionally.

7. To make the sauce, cut the ends off the onion, peel it and slice it. Melt the butter over a low heat. Cook the onion for five minutes.

8. Stir in the flour and cook it for one minute. Take the pan off the heat and add a little of the milk. Stir it really well.

9. Carry on stirring in the milk, a little at a time. Then, stir in the water you saved from cooking the vegetables.

10. Put the pan back onto the heat. Bring the sauce to the boil slowly, stirring all the time. Let the sauce boil for one minute.

11. Grease the dish with margarine. Spoon in the vegetables and sprinkle on some pepper. Pour the sauce over the vegetables.

12. To make the crumble, shake the flour through a sieve into a large bowl. Cut the butter into small chunks. Add it to the bowl.

13. Rub the butter into the flour with your fingertips. Lift it up and let it fall as you do it. Carry on until it looks like breadcrumbs.

14. Stir in the oats and nuts. Use a spoon to sprinkle the crumble evenly over the vegetables to cover them.

15. Bake the crumble in the oven for 35 minutes. The topping will turn golden brown. Spoon it onto plates and eat while it's hot.

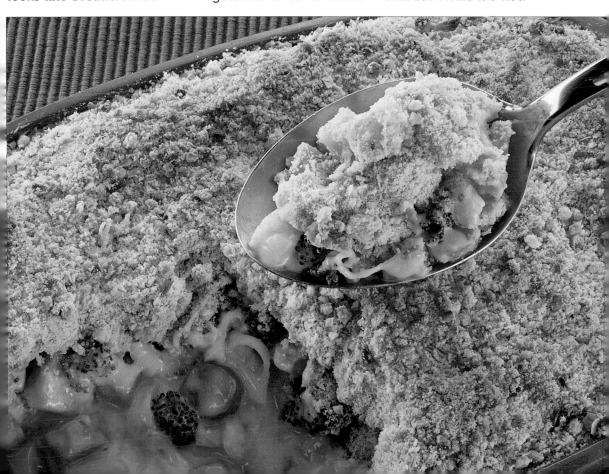

Healthy eating

It's important that you eat a well-balanced diet. This means that you should eat a mixture of things like bread, milk, cheese, eggs, peas, beans and lentils, as well as lots of fruit and vegetables. Try to eat food from the following groups each day. All the food you eat contains substances called nutrients, which keep your body healthy. These are proteins, carbohydrates, fats, vitamins and minerals. You also need fibre and water.

Food	Nutrients
Group 1 : soya milk or cow's milk, cheese, eggs or soya products, such as tofu and soya mince.	protein and minerals, especially calcium
Group 2 : pulses, such as, kidney beans, baked beans, chick peas, lentils; nuts such as almonds, walnuts, hazelnuts, sesame seeds, sunflower seeds.	protein, carbohydrates, fibre, vitamins and minerals
Group 3 : vegetable oil, margarine, butter.	vitamins, fat
Group 4 : bread, pasta, rice, potatoes, wheat products, including flour.	carbohydrates, fibre, vitamins and minerals
Group 5: Fruit and vegetables, including dried fruit, frozen and canned vegetables.	vitamin C, fibre and minerals
Group 6 : eggs, cheese, yeast extract, fortified soya milk, fortified breakfast cereals.	vitamin B. You should eat a little of one of these each day, especially if you eat a vegan diet (see page 98).

A well-balanced meal

Most of the dishes in this book are made up of different types of nutrients, making them well-balanced meals. They contain types of food from the different groups above.

For example, the 'Tortillas with black bean sauce', on page 136, contain beans from group 2, cheese from groups 1 and 6, and tomatoes from group 5. The tortillas are made from flour which is in group 4. However, the dish doesn't contain many fresh vegetables, so it would be a good idea to serve the tortillas with a salad and to eat some fruit afterwards.

Here are a few suggestions for making other dishes in the book well-balanced:-

page 6 - serve the tomato and mozzarella salad with bread, such as the Italian bread on pages 108-109. Eat some dried raisins or apricots afterwards.

pages 122-123 - serve the cheesy sausages with some green vegetables, such as broccoli, green beans, peas or a green salad.

pages 134-135 - serve the vegetarian sausages with baked beans.

CAKES
& COOKIES
FOR BEGINNERS

Before you bake

Before you start to bake, have a look at the tips on these two pages. Don't forget to check that you have all the ingredients and equipment you need before you begin.

In most types of cooking, it doesn't matter if you change an ingredient or leave something out, but you can't do this when you are baking. It's also important that you measure things exactly and use the right size of tin. Otherwise your cakes or cookies may not turn out correctly.

Take butter or margarine out of the fridge at least 30 minutes before you use it, unless the recipe says something different.

Always use medium-sized eggs unless the recipe says something else.

When you measure with a spoon, use a level spoonful, not a heaped one.

Equipment

If you are making a cake, use the size and shape of tin written in the recipe. If you use a different size, you may not have the correct amount of mixture.

Baking sheets

All the cookies are baked on baking sheets. Space out the uncooked cookies, as they usually increase in size as they cook. When you use two baking sheets, put them into your oven one above the other. Cook the top one for the time the recipe says, then take it out. Move the bottom one up and cook until it's ready.

Your oven

It's important that you turn on your oven when the recipe says, so that it heats up. Remember, if you have a fan oven you'll need to lower the temperature or shorten the cooking time. Look in its instruction book to see what is recommended.

Preparing cake tins

You need to grease a cake tin or baking sheet to stop the cake or cookie mixture from sticking to it when it's cooked. In some recipes you also need to line the tin with baking parchment, greaseproof or rice paper, or sprinkle it with flour.

Grease the sides too.

To grease a tin, dip a paper towel into soft butter or margarine. Rub the towel over the bottom.

Which shelf?

Cook your cake or cookies on a shelf in the middle of your oven unless the recipe says something different. Always move the shelf to the middle before you turn on your oven. Don't leave an empty shelf above it.

Cooling

Make sure that you always wear oven gloves when you take anything out of the oven. Leave cakes or cookies in their tin or on the baking sheets for several minutes to cool. Then, put them on a wire rack to cool down completely.

To remove a cake from a loose-bottomed cake tin, put the tin onto a can. Press on the side of the tin so that it slides down.

To turn a cake out of a cake tin, put a wire rack on top of the tin. Turn it over so that the cake comes out.

Baking tips

These pages give you lots of cooking hints and tips that will help you bake successfully. You'll also find other hints with some of the recipes.

Breaking an egg

1. Crack the egg sharply on the rim of a cup or bowl. Push your thumbs into the crack in the shell and pull the sides apart.

2. Before you add an egg to a mixture, break the egg into a separate cup or bowl. It helps you to pick out any shell which may fall in.

Separating eggs

Don't let the yolk break.

Leave the yolk on the saucer.

Egg whites will not whisk if the bowl or whisk are greasy.

1. You will need a bowl and a saucer for this. Crack the egg on the side of the bowl, then pour it slowly onto the saucer.

2. Carefully put an egg cup over the yolk. Tip the saucer over the bowl so that the egg white dribbles into it.

If you are whisking the egg whites, make sure that your bowl and whisk are clean and dry before you start (see page 173).

Beating eggs

Beat with the fork like this.

Beating a cake mixture

If you are beating eggs, you can use a fork instead of a whisk. Beat them until the white and yolk are mixed together.

1. Before you begin to beat, put your bowl on a damp dishcloth. This will stop the bowl from slipping as you beat.

2. Stir the mixture briskly with a wooden spoon or a whisk. You are trying to make a smooth, creamy cake mixture.

Sifting flour

Shake the sieve until all the flour falls through.

Put a sieve over a bowl and pour the flour into it. It you sift wholemeal flour, tip any bran left in the sieve into the bowl.

Rubbing in

1. Cut the butter or margarine into small pieces and stir it into the flour. Stir until each piece is covered with flour.

Do this with clean, dry hands.

2. Rub the pieces with your fingertips. Lift the mixture and let it fall as you rub. Do this until it becomes like fine breadcrumbs.

Rolling out dough

1. Sprinkle a clean, dry work surface with a little flour. Put the dough onto it, then sprinkle a rolling pin with some flour.

2. Press the rolling pin onto the dough and roll it away from you. Turn the dough in a quarter turn and roll it again.

Shape the dough with your hands to keep it circular.

3. Carry on rolling and turning to make a circle, until you get the thickness of dough written in the recipe.

Melting chocolate

1. Heat about 2.5cm (1in) of water in a pan so that it is bubbling gently. Break the chocolate into a heatproof bowl.

Stir the chocolate as it melts.

2. Put on some oven gloves and lift the bowl into the pan. The heat from the water melts the chocolate gradually.

Testing a cake

At the end of the cooking time, test your cake to see if it is cooked. Press it in the middle. If it is cooked, it will feel firm and spring up.

Peanut butter cookies

Makes 12 cookies

50g (2oz) butter or margarine
75g (3oz) soft light brown sugar
100g (4oz) crunchy peanut butter
50g (2oz) self-raising flour
50g (2oz) rolled oats
1 medium egg

For the topping:
  50g (2oz) roasted,
    unsalted peanuts

1. Grease two baking sheets with butter or margarine. Turn the oven on to 170°C, 325°F, Gas mark 3, to heat up.

2. Put the margarine or butter into a large bowl. Add the sugar and peanut butter. Beat them until they are light and creamy.

3. Put a sieve over the bowl and sift the flour onto the mixture. Add the oats and stir well to mix everything together.

4. Press the mixture with your fingers, then fold it in half and press again. Do this again and again until it makes a soft dough.

5. Divide the mixture in half, then in quarters until you make 12 pieces. Squeeze each piece to make a small ball.

6. Put the balls onto the baking sheets, leaving plenty of space between them. Flatten them slightly with your hand.

7. Break the egg into a small bowl and beat it well with a fork. Brush the top of each cookie with some beaten egg.

8. Cut the roasted peanuts into small pieces. Sprinkle them all over the top of each cookie. They will stick to the egg.

9. Bake the cookies for 15 minutes, until they are golden. Leave them on the trays to cool a little, then lift them onto a wire rack.

Corn flake crunch

Makes 8 pieces

225g (8oz) plain chocolate
3 tablespoons of golden
or maple syrup
50g (2oz) margarine
100g (4oz) corn flakes

a 20cm (8in) shallow tin

1. Grease the tin with a little butter or margarine on kitchen paper. Grease the inside well, but do not leave on too much butter.

2. Break the chocolate into a large pan. Add the syrup and margarine. Heat the pan gently, stirring all the time.

Lift the pieces out with a blunt knife or a pie slice.

3. When the chocolate has melted, add the corn flakes and stir them well. Make sure that they are coated all over with chocolate.

4. Spoon the mixture into the tin. Gently smooth the top with the back of a spoon. Try not to crush the corn flakes.

5. Put the tin in a fridge for the chocolate to set. It will take about two hours. Use a sharp knife to cut it into eight pieces.

Marshmallow crispies

Makes 15 pieces

100g (4oz) wrapped toffees or slab toffee
100g (4oz) margarine
100g (4oz) marshmallows
100g (4oz) rice crispies

a shallow tin 27.5 x 17.5cm (11 x 7in)

1. Grease the tin (see page 147). If you are using a slab of toffee, put it in a plastic bag and break it up with a rolling pin.

They will take about 15 minutes to melt.

2. Put the toffee, margarine and marshmallows into a large pan. Melt them very gently over a low heat, stirring all the time.

3. When everything has melted and blended together, take the pan off the heat. Gently stir in the rice crispies.

4. Spoon the mixture into the tin and press it gently with the back of a metal spoon. Leave the mixture to set, then cut it up.

Chocolate chip cookies

Makes 12

100g (4oz) butter or margarine
100g (4oz) caster sugar
1 egg
half a teaspoon of vanilla essence
175g (6oz) plain flour
175g (6oz) chocolate chips

Use a wooden spoon.

1. Grease two large baking sheets with butter or margarine (see page 147). Turn your oven on to 180°C, 350°F, Gas mark 4.

2. Put the sugar and the butter or margarine into a large bowl. Beat it briskly until it is light and creamy (see page 148).

Press down on each cookie.

3. Break the egg into a small bowl and beat it well. Stir in the vanilla essence, then add the mixture to the large bowl.

4. Sift the flour into the large bowl and stir well to make a smooth mixture. Stir in 100g (4oz) of the chocolate chips.

5. Put a heaped tablespoon of the mixture onto a baking sheet. Use up the rest of the mixture to make eleven more cookies.

6. Flatten each cookie slightly with the back of a fork. Sprinkle the top of each one with some of the remaining chocolate chips.

7. Bake the cookies for 10-15 minutes. They should be pale golden brown and slightly soft in the middle.

8. Leave the cookies for a few minutes, then use a spatula or fish slice to lift them onto a wire rack. Leave them to cool.

Hazelnut cookies

Makes 15

150g (5oz) butter or margarine
100g (4oz) caster sugar
1 egg
175g (6oz) plain flour
25g (1oz) cocoa powder
75g (3oz) hazelnuts

You could press a whole hazelnut into the middle of the cookies before you bake them.

1. Follow steps 1-3 of the chocolate chip cookies, using the quantities shown above. You don't add any vanilla at step 3.

2. Sieve the flour and the cocoa powder into the bowl. Use a large spoon to stir it in well, until you get a smooth mixture.

Flatten them with the back of a spoon.

3. Put the hazelnuts onto a chopping board and cut them into pieces. Add them to the mixture and stir them in.

4. Put 15 heaped dessert spoonfuls of the mixture onto the baking sheets. Space them out. Flatten each one a little.

5. Bake the cookies for 10-15 minutes. They will darken. Leave them to cool a little, then lift them onto a wire rack.

Shortbread

Makes 8 pieces

150g (5oz) plain flour
25g (1oz) rice flour or ground rice
100g (4oz) butter, refrigerated
50g (2oz) caster sugar

a 20cm (8in) shallow tin

1. Turn your oven to 150°C, 300°F, Gas mark 2. Grease the inside of the tin with butter on a piece of kitchen paper.

2. Put a sieve over a large mixing bowl and pour the flour and the ground rice into it. Shake them into the bowl.

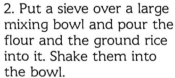

3. Cut the butter into small pieces and put them into the bowl. Mix them with a blunt knife to coat them with flour.

4. Rub the pieces of butter between your fingertips. Lift the mixture and let it fall back into the bowl as you rub (see page 149).

5. Carry on rubbing in the flour until the mixture looks like breadcrumbs. Stir in the caster sugar with a wooden spoon.

6. Holding the bowl in one hand, squeeze the mixture into a ball. The heat from your hand makes the mixture stick together.

Cut across it again, before lifting it out.

7. Press the mixture into the tin with your fingers, then use the back of a spoon to smooth the top and make it level.

8. Use the prongs of a fork to press a pattern around the edge. Then cut the mixture into eight equal pieces.

9. Bake it for 30 minutes, until it becomes golden. Leave the shortbread for five minutes before putting it on a wire rack.

Gingerbread biscuits

Makes about 20 biscuits

350g (12oz) plain flour
2 teaspoons of ground ginger
1 teaspoon of bicarbonate of soda
100g (4oz) butter or margarine
175g (6oz) soft light brown sugar
1 egg
4 tablespoons of golden syrup or
    maple syrup

large cookie cutters

1. Dip a paper towel in some margarine and rub it over two baking sheets. Turn on your oven to 190°C, 375°F, Gas mark 5.

Look at the tip for measuring syrup, below right.

2. Sift the flour, ginger and bicarbonate of soda into a mixing bowl. Cut the butter or margarine into chunks and add them.

3. Rub the butter or margarine into the flour with your fingers, until the mixture looks like fine breadcrumbs (see page 149).

4. Stir the sugar into the mixture. Break the egg into a small bowl. Add the syrup to the egg and beat them together well.

5. Stir the eggy mixture into the flour. Mix everything together with a metal spoon until it makes a dough.

6. Sprinkle a clean work surface with flour and put the dough onto it. Stretch the dough by pushing it away from you.

7. Fold the dough in half. Turn it and push it away from you again. Continue to push, turn and fold until the dough is smooth.

You can use any shape of cutter you like.

8. Cut the dough in half. Sprinkle a little more flour onto your work surface. Roll out the dough until it is about 5mm (¼in) thick.

Spread the shapes out on the baking sheet.

9. Use a cookie cutter to cut out lots of shapes from the dough. Lift the shapes onto the baking sheets with a fish slice.

10. Roll out the other half of dough and cut shapes from it. Squeeze the scraps of dough to make a ball. Roll it out and cut more shapes.

11. Put the biscuits on the baking sheets into your oven and bake them for 12-15 minutes. They will turn golden brown.

12. Leave the biscuits on the sheets for about five minutes. Then, lift them onto a wire rack. Leave them to cool.

Measuring syrup

Heat your spoon in hot water before you measure syrup. It makes it easier for the syrup to slide off.

Flapjacks

Makes 12

175g (6oz) margarine
175g (6oz) Demerara sugar
2 tablespoons of golden syrup
225g (8oz) rolled oats or porridge oats

a shallow 18 x 27cm (7 x 11in) tin

1. Put the tin on baking parchment or greaseproof paper and draw around it. Cut out the oblong just inside the line.

Cut the flapjacks while they are in the tin and still warm.

Grease the tin well.

2. Grease the bottom of the cake tin and put the paper in. Grease the paper. Turn on your oven to 160°C, 325°F, Gas mark 3.

3. Put the margarine in a large pan with the sugar and syrup. Melt the margarine gently. Do not allow the mixture to boil.

4. Take the pan off the heat. Add the oats and stir them in really well so that they are covered in the margarine mixture.

5. Spoon the oats into the tin. Spread them all over the bottom, then smooth the top with the back of a metal spoon.

6. Put the tin on the middle shelf in your oven and bake the mixture for 25 minutes until the oats turn golden brown.

7. Take the tin out of the oven and leave it for ten minutes. Cut the mixture into pieces. Leave them in the tin until they are cold.

Chocolate refrigerator cake

Makes about 12 slices

100g (4oz) bar of plain chocolate,
Or, 100g (4oz) bar of white chocolate
100g (4oz) butter or margarine
5 tablespoons of golden syrup
225g (8oz) rich tea biscuits
2 tablespoons of chopped glacé cherries
2 tablespoons of raisins
2 tablespoons of chopped nuts

a 20cm (8in) round tin

Find out how to grease a tin on page 147.

Use white or plain chocolate for this recipe.

1. Put your cake tin onto greaseproof paper and draw around it. Cut out the circle, just inside the line you have drawn.

2. Grease the tin. Put in the greaseproof paper circle you have cut out. Grease it again, on top of the paper circle.

3. Break the chocolate into pieces and put it in a saucepan. Add the butter or margarine and spoon in the syrup.

4. Put the pan over a low heat and let the mixture melt. Stir it occasionally. When the mixture has melted, turn off the heat.

5. Break the biscuits into pieces and put them into a bowl. Crush the pieces of biscuit finely with the end of a rolling pin.

6. Put the chopped glacé cherries, raisins and chopped nuts into the bowl. Add the mixture from the pan and stir well.

7. Spoon the mixture into the cake tin. Press it down really well, then smooth the top with the back of a metal spoon.

8. Put the tin into a fridge and leave it overnight. Turn the cake out and pull off the paper circle. Cut the cake into wedges.

Macaroons

Makes 12

3 large eggs (you only need the whites)
12 whole blanched almonds
75g (3oz) caster sugar
100g (4oz) ground almonds
25g (1oz) ground rice
a few drops of almond essence

Grease the top of the paper.

1. Turn your oven on to 150°C, 300°F, Gas mark 2. Cover the baking sheets with either rice paper or baking parchment.

If you don't have rice paper or baking parchment, cover the baking sheets with greaseproof paper. Grease the paper lightly.

Be careful not to break the yolk.

You don't need the yolks.

Lift them out with a teaspoon.

2. Break the egg on the side of a bowl. Hold it over a saucer and pull the sides apart. Let the egg fall gently onto a saucer.

3. Hold an egg cup over the egg yolk and tip the egg white into a large mixing bowl. Do the same with the other eggs.

4. Put the almonds into the egg white, then lift them out with a spoon. Put them on a plate and leave them on one side.

Make sure your whisk is clean and dry before you begin.

Use a metal spoon to fold the mixture (see the tip, page 183).

5. Whisk the egg whites (see the tip, page 173). Stop whisking when you get small points, or 'peaks', when you lift your whisk.

6. Add the caster sugar, ground almonds, ground rice and almond essence. Fold the mixture over and over gently to mix them.

7. Put a heaped teaspoon of the mixture onto the paper on the baking sheet, and flatten it slightly with the back of the spoon.

The macaroons spread as they cook.

You can eat any rice paper left on the bottom.

8. Use up the rest of the mixture in the same way, leaving a space between each spoonful. Press an almond onto each one.

9. Bake the macaroons for 25-30 minutes, until they are pale golden brown. Leave them on the baking sheets for five minutes.

10. Lift the macaroons onto a wire rack to cool. If you have used rice paper, tear away the paper around each macaroon.

Fruity buns

Makes 12 buns

225g (8oz) self-raising flour
100g (4oz) butter or margarine
100g (4oz) caster sugar
1 medium egg
1 tablespoon of milk
50g (2oz) raspberry jam

You don't have to use raspberry jam, you could try different flavours, such as apricot or blackcurrant.

1. Turn your oven on to 200°C, 400°F, Gas mark 6. Grease two baking sheets and sprinkle them with flour. Shake them to spread the flour, then tip it off.

2. Put a sieve over a large bowl and shake the flour through it. Cut the butter or margarine into small chunks and add them to the flour.

3. Rub the chunks of butter or margarine into the flour with your fingers, until it looks like fine breadcrumbs (see page 149). Stir in the sugar.

4. Break the egg into a small bowl and add the milk. Whisk them together, then stir them into the mixture in the large bowl.

5. Sprinkle a clean work surface with some flour. Press the mixture together to make a firm ball, then put it onto your work surface.

Don't try to eat them while they are hot. The jam could burn you.

6. Cut the ball in half. Then, cut each half into three pieces. Cut each of the pieces in half. You should end up with 12 even-sized pieces.

7. Squeeze each piece into a round shape and spread them out on the baking sheets. Make a dent in each bun and fill it with a teaspoon of jam.

8. Bake the buns for ten minutes. They will rise and turn golden brown. Lift each one onto a wire rack and leave them to cool before eating them.

Chocolate choux buns

Makes about 18 buns

150ml (¼ pint) cold water
1 teaspoon caster sugar
50g (2oz) butter
60g (2½oz) plain flour
2 eggs

For the filling:
250ml (½ pint) double cream

For the icing:
225g (8oz) plain chocolate

1. Turn on your oven to 200°C, 400°F, Gas mark 6. Dip a paper towel in some margarine and rub it over two baking sheets.

2. Turn on the cold tap and hold each baking sheet under it. Shake them well to get rid of all the drops of water.

3. Put a sieve over a bowl and pour in the flour. Sift the flour into the bowl. Put this on one side. You'll need it later.

Beat the mixture quickly to mix in all the flour.

4. Put the water, sugar and butter into a large saucepan. Place the pan over a medium heat to melt the butter.

5. As soon as the butter has melted, turn up the heat and bring the mixture to the boil. Then, turn off the heat.

6. Immediately, shoot the flour into the pan in one go, and start to beat the mixture really well with a wooden spoon.

7. Keep beating the mixture until it makes a ball of smooth paste which leaves the sides of the pan clean.

8. Break the eggs into a small bowl and beat them. Add them, a little at a time, beating the mixture each time you add some.

9. Put teaspoonfuls of the mixture onto the baking sheets. Make sure that they are spaced out. They will spread as they cook.

Slit the buns to allow the hot air inside to escape.

10. Bake them for 25-30 minutes, until they are golden brown. Make a slit in each one and leave them on a rack to cool.

11. Whisk the cream until it is stiff. Cut the buns in half. Fill them with a teaspoon of cream, then press them together again.

12. Break the chocolate into chunks and let it melt in a bowl over a saucepan of hot water (see page 149).

13. Using a teaspoon, carefully coat the top of each bun with the melted chocolate. Leave the chocolate to harden.

Scones

Makes 16 scones

225g (8oz) self-raising flour
1 level teaspoon of baking powder
a pinch of salt
50g (2oz) butter or margarine
25g (1oz) caster sugar
150ml (¼ pint) milk
extra milk for brushing

6cm or 7cm (2½in) scone cutter

You can also make fruit scones by adding 50g (2oz) of sultanas, chopped glacé cherries or chopped dates, with the sugar at step 3.

Hold the sieve up above the bowl.

1. Turn your oven on to heat up to 230°C, 450°F, Gas mark 8. Grease two baking sheets with butter or margarine.

2. Sift the flour, baking powder and salt into a bowl. Cut the butter or margarine into small pieces and add them to the flour.

Use your fingertips.

3. Rub the butter or margarine into the flour until the mixture looks like fine breadcrumbs. Add the sugar and milk.

4. Use a blunt knife to mix everything to make a soft dough. Then, press and mould it with your fingers until it's smooth.

5. Sprinkle an area of your work surface with flour and put the dough onto it. Roll it out until the dough is about 1cm (½in) thick.

Cut the circles close together.

6. Cut circles from the dough with the cutter. Squeeze the scraps into a ball and roll them out again. Cut more circles.

7. Put the circles onto the baking sheets, leaving quite a lot of space between each one. Brush the tops with a little milk.

8. Bake the scones for 7-10 minutes on the top shelf of the oven. They will rise and turn golden. Lift them onto a wire rack to cool.

Baked cheesecake squares

Makes 15 squares

225g (8oz) plain flour
100g (4oz) butter
1 tablespoon of caster sugar
2 tablespoons of water

an 18 x 27 x 2.5cm (7 x 11 x 1in) tin

For the filling: 150ml (¼ pint) sour cream
225g (8oz) curd cheese, ricotta cheese
    or quark
50g (2oz) caster sugar
a lemon
3 eggs
50g (2oz) raisins

Rub in the butter until it looks like breadcrumbs.

1. Draw around the tray on baking parchment or greaseproof paper. Cut out the shape. Grease the tray and put the paper into it.

2. Turn your oven on to 200°C, 400°F, Gas mark 6. Sift the flour. Cut the butter into pieces and rub it in (see page 149).

3. Stir in the sugar. Add the water and mix to make a soft dough. Mix it until the mixture leaves the side of the bowl clean.

Beat the mixture until smooth.

4. Put the dough into the tray and press it with your fingers to cover the bottom of the tray. Press it right into the corners.

5. Prick the dough all over with a fork. Bake it for 10 minutes until it is golden. Turn the oven down to 160°C, 325°F, Gas mark 3.

6. Put the sour cream, cheese and caster sugar into a bowl. Grate the yellow rind off the lemon and add it. Beat the mixture well.

Turn the mixture over and over.

7. Separate the eggs (see page 148). Put the whites into a medium-sized bowl. Add the yolks to the mixture and beat it again.

8. Whisk the egg whites until they are stiff (see right). Fold them gently into the mixture with a metal spoon (see page 183).

9. Sprinkle the raisins over the dough and pour the eggy mixture on top. Bake for 45-50 minutes until it is golden brown.

Whisking egg whites

1. Separate the egg whites from their yolks and put them into a clean, dry bowl. Make sure that no yolk gets into the bowl.

2. Hold the bowl tightly in one hand and twist the whisk around and around. The egg will begin to go white and frothy.

3. Carry on whisking until the whites get stiff and you get points or 'peaks' forming on the top when you lift up the whisk.

Chocolate brownies

Makes 15

175g (6oz) margarine
350g (12oz) caster sugar
1 teaspoon of vanilla essence
3 eggs
100g (4oz) plain flour
1 level teaspoon of baking powder
75g (3oz) cocoa
175g (6oz) walnuts or pecan nuts

an oblong tin,
  22 x 30 x 2.5cm (9 x 12 x 1in)

1. Put your cake tin on a piece of greaseproof paper or baking parchment. Draw around it and cut out the shape.

2. Grease the tin. Lay the paper in the tin and grease the top of it. Turn the oven on to 180°C, 350°F, Gas mark 4.

3. Put the margarine into a pan and melt it over a low heat. Pour it into a large mixing bowl, then add the sugar and vanilla essence.

Beat the mixture each time you add some egg.

4. Break the eggs into a small bowl and beat them. Add them to the large bowl, a little at a time. Beat them in well.

5. Sift the flour into the bowl and add the baking powder and the cocoa. Stir everything together so that it is mixed well.

6. Put the nuts onto a chopping board and cut them into small pieces. Add them to the mixture and stir it well again.

7. Pour the mixture into the cake tin and smooth the top with the back of a spoon. Bake it for about 40 minutes.

8. The brownies are ready when they have risen and have formed a crust on top. They should still be soft in the middle.

Use a fish slice to lift them.

9. Leave the brownies in the tin for five minutes, then cut them into 15 squares. Leave them on a wire rack to cool.

Pecan squares

Makes 12 squares

For the base: 175g (6oz) butter or margarine
75g (3oz) icing sugar
225g (8oz) plain flour

For the topping: 75g (3oz) butter or margarine
2 tablespoons of golden or maple syrup
2 tablespoons of milk
1 teaspoon of vanilla essence
50g (2oz) soft brown sugar
2 eggs
100g (4oz) pecan nuts

an oblong tin, 18 x 27 x 2.5cm (7 x 11 x 1in)

1. Put the tin onto a piece of greaseproof paper or baking parchment. Draw around it and cut out the shape you have drawn.

2. Grease the tin. Put the paper into the bottom of the tin and press it down. Turn the oven on to 180°C, 350°F, Gas mark 4.

3. For the base, put the butter or margarine into a mixing bowl. Add the sugar and beat it until it is light and creamy.

4. Sift the flour into the bowl and stir it in well. Sprinkle flour onto a clean work surface and put the mixture onto it.

5. Press the mixture with your fingers, fold it in half, then press again. Do this again and again for about a minute.

6. Use the back of a spoon to press the mixture over the bottom of the tin. Bake it for about 15 minutes or until it is golden brown.

7. When the base has cooked, leave it in the tin, but put it on a wire rack to cool. Begin to make the topping while it cools.

8. Put the butter or margarine into a pan and melt it over a low heat. Stir in the syrup, sugar, milk and vanilla essence.

9. Break the eggs into a small bowl and beat them well. Take the pan off the heat and stir the beaten eggs into the mixture.

10. Pour the topping onto the base. Sprinkle the pecan nuts evenly over the topping and bake it for about 25 minutes.

11. The topping will turn dark golden brown, but it should be slightly gooey in the middle. Leave it to cool in the tin.

12. When it has cooled, cut it into 12 squares, by making two cuts lengthways along the tin, then three cuts across.

Banana and nut slices

Makes 9 slices

100g (4oz) butter or margarine
100g (4oz) soft light brown sugar
2 eggs
2 bananas
100g (4oz) self-raising flour
1 teaspoon of baking powder
100g (4oz) chopped nuts

a 20cm (8in) square cake tin

1. Grease your cake tin with butter or margarine. Carefully follow the instructions on page 179 for lining your cake tin.

2. Turn on your oven to 190°C, 375°F, Gas mark 5. Put the butter or margarine into a mixing bowl. Add the sugar.

3. Use a wooden spoon to beat the butter or margarine and the sugar, until they are very smooth and creamy.

4. Carefully break the eggs into a small bowl. Beat them with a whisk or a fork until they are mixed well (see page 148).

5. Add the beaten egg to the creamy mixture, a little at a time. Each time you add some egg, beat it into the mixture.

6. Peel the bananas. Cut them into chunks, then put them into a bowl. Mash them well with the back of a fork.

7. Stir the mashed banana into the creamy mixture. Put a sieve over the bowl and sift the flour and baking powder into it.

8. Use a metal spoon to stir the flour into the mixture. Do this by turning the mixture over slowly with the spoon.

9. Spoon the mixture into your cake tin. Sprinkle the top with the chopped nuts and bake it for about 20-25 minutes.

10. Press lightly on the top of the cake to test it. It should spring back up. Leave it to cool in the tin for five minutes.

11. Hold the greaseproof paper and lift the cake out of the tin. Leave it on a wire rack to cool, then cut it into slices.

Greasing & lining a tin

Put the tin on a piece of baking parchment or greaseproof paper which is larger than the tin.

Use a pencil to draw around the tin, as close to the bottom as you can. Lift the tin off.

Cut in from the edge to each corner of the square. Fold in each side along its pencil line.

Grease the tin. Fit the paper into the tin. Trim off any extra paper, just above the tin.

Simple sponge cakes

Makes 18 squares. Ice the cakes with sugar icing or butter cream icing.

For the squares: 275g (10oz) self-raising flour
225g (8oz) soft margarine
4 tablespoons of milk
1 level teaspoon of baking powder
225g (8oz) caster sugar
2-3 drops of vanilla essence
4 eggs

For sugar icing: 225g (8oz) icing sugar
about 2 tablespoons of water

For butter cream icing:
75g (3oz) butter, softened
175g (6oz) icing sugar
1 teaspoon of vanilla essence

For decorating: small sweets

a 33 x 25cm (13 x 10in) roasting tin

Find out about greasing on page 147.

Use a wooden spoon.

1. Grease the tin. Draw around it on baking parchment or greaseproof paper. Cut out the shape and put it in the tin.

2. Turn the oven on to 180°C, 350°F, Gas mark 4. Put a sieve over a large mixing bowl and sift the flour through it.

3. Add the margarine, milk, baking powder, sugar and vanilla. Break the eggs into a small bowl, then add them too. Beat everything well.

Leave the cake in the tin to cool.

4. Scrape the mixture into the tin and smooth the top. Bake it for 40-45 minutes, until the cake springs up when you press the middle.

5. Make the icing when the cake has cooled completely. For sugar icing: sift the icing sugar into a bowl. Add a little water and stir.

Add some more water and stir it again. Continue to do this until the icing coats the back of the spoon and dribbles off it.

For butter cream icing: beat the butter in a bowl until it is creamy. Sift in the icing sugar. Add the vanilla and mix it well.

6. Lift the cake out of the tin, then spread the icing over it. Cut the cake into squares and decorate each piece before the icing sets.

Variations

Cherry and coconut: add 175g (6oz) chopped glacé cherries and 75g (3oz) desiccated coconut to the mixture at step 3.

Chocolate: add 2 tablespoons of cocoa powder to the mixture at step 3. Leave out the vanilla essence.

Lemon: grate the rind off two lemons and add it to the mixture at step 3. Leave out the vanilla essence.

Marble cake

Makes about 8 slices

225g (8oz) butter or margarine
225g (8oz) caster sugar
4 eggs
225g (8oz) self-raising flour

an orange
2 tablespoons of cocoa powder

a tin measuring 20.5 x 12.5 x 8cm
(8 x 5 x 3½ in)

1. Put the tin onto some greaseproof paper or baking parchment and draw around the bottom. Cut out the shape.

2. Grease inside the tin, then put the paper into the bottom. Turn the oven on to 180°C, 350°F, Gas mark 4.

3. Put the butter or margarine and the sugar into a mixing bowl. Beat them until they are mixed well and creamy.

Beat well each time you add some egg.

Use the medium holes on your grater.

4. Break the eggs into a small bowl and beat them. Add the beaten egg, a little at a time, to the creamy mixture.

5. Sift the flour into the bowl, then 'fold' it in with a metal spoon (see tip, right). Divide the mixture between two bowls.

6. Grate the yellow rind off the orange. Take care not to grate any of the white part under the skin, as it tastes bitter.

7. Add the orange rind to one bowl and the cocoa powder to the other. Stir each bowl well, using separate spoons.

8. Put alternate spoonfuls of the mixture into the tin. Use a knife to make swirly patterns through the mixture. Smooth the top.

9. Bake the cake for an hour to an hour and 20 minutes. The cake should be well-risen and firm when you press it.

Folding in

You'll see the marble effect when you cut the cake.

10. Leave the cake in the tin for 10 minutes to cool, then turn it onto a wire rack. When it is cold, cut it into slices.

Use a metal spoon to cut through the middle of the mixture, then fold it over very gently. Do this again and again.

Carry on cutting and folding until the ingredients are mixed. Folding in keeps your mixture very light.

Layered lemon cake

Makes about 12 slices

a lemon
175g (6oz) self-raising flour
1 teaspoon of baking powder
3 eggs
175g (6oz) soft margarine
175g (6oz) caster sugar

For the filling:
2 eggs
75g (3oz) caster sugar

a lemon
50g (2oz) unsalted butter

For the icing:
a lemon
100g (4oz) icing sugar

two round 18cm (7in) tins

Heat your oven to 180°C, 350°F,
Gas mark 4.

Put a circle in the bottom of each tin.

Use the medium holes on the grater.

1. Turn on your oven. Draw around the tins on baking parchment or greaseproof paper. Cut out the circles. Grease the tins.

2. Grate the rind off a lemon, then cut the lemon in half. Twist each half on a lemon squeezer to get the juice from it.

3. Sift the flour and baking powder into a bowl. Break the eggs into a cup, then add them, along with the margarine and sugar.

Smooth the top with a spoon.

4. Beat everything in the bowl well, then stir in the lemon rind and juice. Divide the mixture between the two tins.

5. Bake the cakes for 25 minutes until they spring up when you press them in the middle. Leave them on a rack to cool.

6. While the cakes are cooling, make the filling. Break the eggs into a heatproof bowl and add the caster sugar.

Wear oven gloves.

It will take about 20 minutes.

7. Add the grated rind and juice of another lemon. Cut the butter into small pieces and add it to the bowl.

8. Put some water into a pan and turn on the heat so that the water is just bubbling. Put the bowl into the pan.

9. Stir the mixture from time to time as it thickens. Take it off the heat when it coats the back of your spoon. Leave it to cool.

Leave the cake on the rack.

A zester gives you long pieces of rind.

Press hard as you scrape.

Stir in the juice a little at a time.

10. Spread one cake with the filling. Put the other cake carefully on top. Don't worry if some of the filling oozes out.

11. Either grate some rind from the last lemon or scrape some off with a zester, if you have one. Keep it on one side.

12. Squeeze one half of the lemon. Sift the icing sugar. Stir the juice into the icing until it is like glue. Ice the cake. Sprinkle rind on top.

Apple cake

Makes about 12 slices

175g (6oz) wholemeal self-raising flour
175g (6oz) caster sugar
1 teaspoon of baking powder
3 eggs
175g (6oz) soft margarine

1 rounded teaspoon of ground cinnamon
50g (2oz) chopped nuts
1 cooking apple, about 225g (8oz)
Demerara sugar for sprinkling on top

a 20cm (8in) round, loose-bottomed
    cake tin

1. Put the cake tin onto some greaseproof paper or baking parchment. Draw around it and cut out the circle, just inside the line.

2. Grease the tin with some margarine, then put the paper into the bottom of it. Turn the oven on to 170°C, 325°F, Gas mark 3.

3. Sift the flour into a large bowl and tip in the grainy bits left in the bottom of your sieve. Add the caster sugar and baking powder.

This cake is delicious if you eat it while it is still slightly warm.

4. Break the eggs into a small bowl, then add them to the bowl along with the margarine, cinnamon and half of the nuts.

5. Use a wooden spoon to mix everything together really well. Spoon the mixture into the tin and smooth the top.

6. Peel the apple (see tip), then cut out the core. Cut the apple into thin slices. Lay the slices in circles on top, overlapping each one.

7. Sprinkle the apples with the remaining nuts and a tablespoon of Demerara sugar. Bake the cake for an hour, until it is firm.

Peeling apples

Put it on a wire rack to cool.

8. Leave the cake in the tin for ten minutes, before slipping off the ring of the tin and lifting the cake off the base. Leave it to cool.

Hold the apple in one hand. Scrape a vegetable peeler towards you again and again to remove the skin.

Apricot and orange loaf

Makes about 8 slices

100g (4oz) ready-to-eat dried apricots
an orange
100g (4oz) self-raising flour
100g (4oz) soft margarine
100g (4oz) light soft brown sugar
2 eggs

For the icing:
100g (4oz) icing sugar
2 tablespoons of orange juice

a loaf tin measuring 20.5 x 12.5 x 8cm
(8 x 5 x 3½in)

1. Put the loaf tin onto baking parchment or greaseproof paper. Draw around the bottom of the tin and cut out the shape.

2. Grease the tin and put the paper into the bottom. Turn your oven on to heat up to 180°C, 350°F, Gas mark 4.

3. Use kitchen scissors to snip the dried apricots into small pieces. Cut them so that they fall into a large mixing bowl.

Use the medium holes on your grater.

Tilt the bowl slightly as you beat.

4. Grate the rind off the orange. Try not to grate any of the white pith underneath. Scrape the rind into the bowl.

5. Sift the flour into the bowl. Add the margarine and brown sugar. Break the eggs into a cup, then pour them in too.

6. Put the bowl onto a damp dishcloth. Beat the mixture firmly with a wooden spoon, until it is light and fluffy.

7. Scrape the mixture out of the bowl into the loaf tin. Smooth the top with the back of a spoon to make it level.

8. Bake the loaf for about 40 minutes, until it rises and turns golden. Leave it for a few minutes, then turn it onto a wire rack.

Pour on the icing when the loaf is cool.

9. Sieve the icing sugar into a bowl. Mix in some orange juice, a little at a time, until it is like runny glue. Pour it over the loaf.

Chocolate cobweb cake

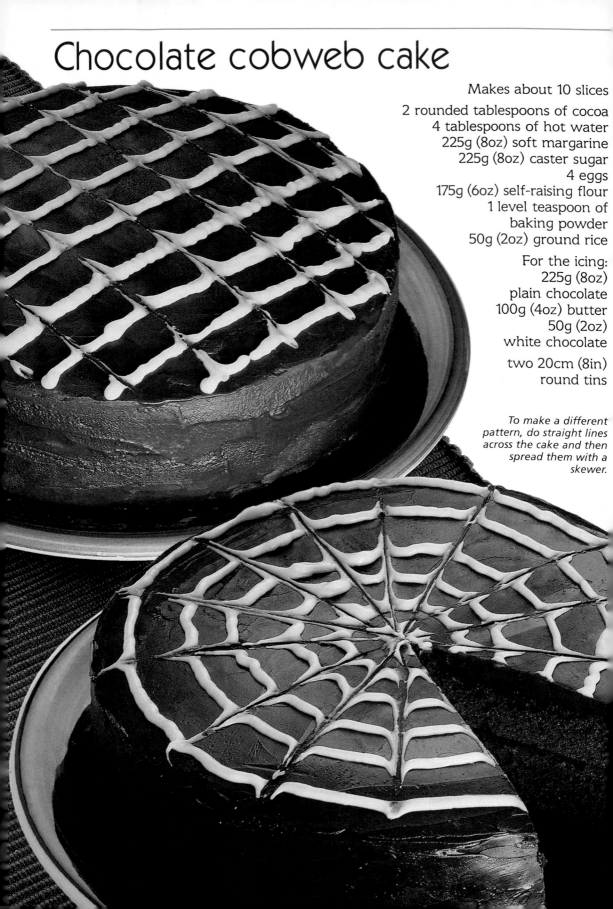

Makes about 10 slices

2 rounded tablespoons of cocoa
4 tablespoons of hot water
225g (8oz) soft margarine
225g (8oz) caster sugar
4 eggs
175g (6oz) self-raising flour
1 level teaspoon of
baking powder
50g (2oz) ground rice

For the icing:
225g (8oz)
plain chocolate
100g (4oz) butter
50g (2oz)
white chocolate

two 20cm (8in)
round tins

*To make a different
pattern, do straight lines
across the cake and then
spread them with a
skewer.*

Make sure that the circles lie flat.

1. Draw around the tins on baking parchment or greaseproof paper. Cut out the circles. Grease the tins and put a circle in each one.

2. Turn your oven on to 180°C, 350°F, Gas mark 4. Put the cocoa into a small bowl. Add the hot water and mix until it's smooth.

3. Put the margarine, sugar, eggs, flour, baking powder and ground rice into a large bowl. Beat well, then stir in the cocoa mixture.

Smooth the top with a spoon.

4. Put half the mixture into each tin. Bake the cakes for 25 minutes until they rise. Turn them out onto a wire rack to cool.

5. For the icing, melt the plain chocolate in a bowl over a pan of hot water (see page 149). Cut up the butter and mix it in well.

6. Turn one cake flat-side up and spread on half of the icing. Put the other cake on top. Cover the top and sides with the rest of the icing.

Get someone to help you spoon in the chocolate.

7. Break the white chocolate into pieces and put it in a heatproof bowl. Melt it over a pan of hot water. Stir as it melts.

8. Leave the chocolate for five minutes, then take two small plastic bags and put one inside the other. Spoon in the chocolate.

9. Hold the bag over a plate and snip off a tiny corner. Be careful or the chocolate will start to run out immediately.

Tilt the bag between each circle to stop the chocolate running out.

10. Gently squeeze the bag as you draw a circle in the middle of the cake. Add more circles around it.

11. Drag a skewer or the tip of a knife from the centre out to the edge. Do this several times to make a cobweb pattern.

Index

The sign (v) after a page number, means that the recipe is vegetarian. If it has an asterisk too, (v)*, the recipe is suitable for vegans (see page 98).

adding salt and pepper, 4
apple cake, 186 (v)
apple pizza, 94 (v)
apricot and orange loaf, 188 (v)

bacon and chicken pasta, 68
baked,
    cheesecake squares, 172 (v)
    eggs, 132 (v)
    Spanish omelette, 126 (v)
baking,
    sheets, 146
    tips, 148
banana and nut slices, 178 (v)
bean,
    dip, 102 (v)
    sauce, with tortillas, 136 (v)
    soup, Mexican, 110 (v)*
beating,
    a mixture, 4
    eggs, 148
beef,
    burgers, 10
    goulash with tagliatelle, 32
biscuits, gingerbread, 158 (v)
black bean sauce with tortillas, 136 (v)
bolognese sauce, with penne, 60
bolognese sauce, soya, 114 (v)*
bread,
    and cheese pudding, 104 (v)
    Italian, 108 (v)
    pizzas, 18
breadcrumbs, making, 100
breadsticks, 103 (v)*
breaking eggs, 133
buns,
    chocolate choux, 168 (v)
    fruity, 166 (v)
burgers,
    cheesy beef, 10
    veggie, 118 (v)*

cake,
    apple, 186, (v)
    carrot, 44 (v)
    chocolate cobweb, 190 (v)
    chocolate refrigerator, 162 (v)

cake, continued,
    gooey chocolate fudge, 42 (v)
    layered lemon, 184 (v)
    marble, 182 (v)
    testing, 149
cake tins,
    lining, 179
    preparing and greasing, 147
cakes,
    simple sponge, 180 (v)
calzones (folded pizzas), 92
carbonara, spaghetti alla, 54
cauliflower, cutting, 125
cheese,
    adding cheese to a sauce, 59
    and bread pudding, 104 (v)
    and tomato tart, 116 (v)
    bites with tomato sauce, 128 (v)
    crunchies, 101 (v)
    grating, 4
    macaroni, 58 (v)
    omelette, 14 (v)
cheesecake,
    lemon and honey, 36
    squares, baked, 172 (v)
cheesy,
    beef burgers, 10
    sausages, 122 (v)
    spinach flan, 20 (v)
    tortellini, 65
Chicago pizza pie, 86
chicken,
    and bacon pasta, 68
    pan-fried, 22
    roast, with vegetables, 34
chocolate,
    brownies, 174 (v)
    chip cookies, 154 (v)
    choux buns, 168 (v)
    cobweb cake, 190 (v)
    fudge cake, 42 (v)
    melting, 149
    refrigerator cake, 162 (v)
chopping,
    an onion, 5
    parsley, 9
chunky vegetable goulash, 124 (v)
cleaning mushrooms, 51
cookies, 46 (v)
    hazelnut, 155 (v)
    peanut butter, 150 (v)
cooking pasta, 53

cooling cakes and cookies, 147
corn flake crunch, 152 (v)
courgette and tomato pizza, 90 (v)
cracked wheat risotto, 112 (v)*
creamy fish pie, 12
croustade, mushroom, 120 (v)
crumble,
    fudgey fruit, 38 (v)
    nut, 142 (v)
crunchies, cheese, 101 (v)
crunchy cheese omelette, 14 (v)
crushing garlic, 5, 55
crusty bread 'pizzas', 18
cutting,
    cauliflower, 125
    peppers, 100

dough,
    kneading, 79
    patterns, 93
    pizza, 78, 82

eggs,
    baked, 132 (v)
    beating, 148
    breaking, 133
    cheese omelette, 14 (v)
    separating, 148
    Spanish omelette, 126 (v)
    whisking whites, 173

filo pastry, using, 141
fish, pan-fried, 22
fish pie, 12
flan, cheesy spinach, 20 (v)
flapjacks, 160 (v)
florets, cauliflower and broccoli, 98
folded pizzas (calzones), 92
folding in, 183
fruit crumble, fudgey, 38 (v)
fruity buns, 166 (v)
fudgey fruit crumble, 38 (v)

garlic, preparing, 5
gingerbread biscuits, 158 (v)
gooey chocolate fudge cake, 42 (v)
goulash,
    beef, with tagliatelle, 32
    chunky vegetable, 124 (v)
grated mozzarella cheese, 51
grating cheese, 4
greasing and lining a cake tin, 179

hazelnut cookies, 155 (v)
healthy eating, 144
honey, measuring, 37
hot apple pizza, 94 (v)

Italian bread, 108 (v)

kebabs, lamb, in pitta pockets, 24
kneading dough, 79

lamb kebabs in pitta pockets, 24
layered lemon cake, 184 (v)
leek and potato soup, 8 (v)
leeks, preparing, 98, 122
lemon,
    and honey cheesecake, 36
    cake, layered, 184 (v)
lining and greasing a cake tin, 179

macaroni cheese, 58 (v)
macaroons, 164 (v)
making,
    breadcrumbs, 100
    stock, 61
Margherita pizza, 82 (v)
marshmallow crispies, 153
measuring,
    honey, 37
    liquids, 48
    solids, 48
    syrup, 159
    with a spoon, 3
meat, pan-fried, 22
meatballs in tomato sauce, 70
Mexican bean soup, 110 (v)*
minestrone soup, 72
mini pizzas, 84
mozzarella and tomato salad, 6 (v)
mozzarella cheese, 51
mushroom,
    and garlic pasta, 56 (v)
    croustade, 120 (v)
mushrooms, preparing, 51

Neapolitan pizza, 80
noodles with tofu skewers, 130 (v)
nut,
    and banana slices, 178 (v)
    crumble, 142 (v)

omelette,
    baked Spanish, 126 (v)

omelette, continued
   crunchy cheese, 14 (v)
onions,
   chopping, 5
   softening, 111
orange and apricot loaf, 188 (v)
oven, 2

pancakes, stuffed, 16
pan-fried meat or fish, 22
parsley, chopping, 9
pasta,
   how to cook, 53
   shapes, 96
   types of, 52, 53, 96
pasta sauces,
   alla carbonara, 54
   bolognese, 60
   bolognese, soya, 144 (v)*
   carbonara, 54
   cheese, 58 (v)
   chicken and bacon, 68
   garlic mushroom, 56 (v)
   fresh tomato, 28 (v)
   green vegetables, 62
   spicy sausage, 57
   tomato, 64, 70, 80
peanut butter cookies, 150 (v)
pecan squares, 176 (v)
peeling,
   apples, 187
   potatoes, 4
penne with bolognese sauce, 60
peppers,
   cutting, 100
   stuffed, 138 (v)
pilaff, prawn and pepper, 30
pizza bases, 50
   making, 78
   scone, 82
   traditional, 78
pizza,
   apple, 94 (v)
   bread, 18
   calzones, (folded pizzas), 92
   Chicago, pie, 86
   courgette and tomato pizza, 90 (v)
   Margherita, 82 (v)
   mini, 84
   Neapolitan, 80
   prawn, 88
   tomato and courgette, 90 (v)

potato and leek soup, 8 (v)
prawn and pepper pilaff, 30
prawn pizza, 88
pudding, bread and cheese, 104 (v)

quick Margherita pizza, 82 (v)

ravioli with tomato sauce, 64
refrigerator cake, chocolate, 162
rice,
   cooking, 107
   tropical spiced, 106 (v)*
ricotta and spinach pasta shells, 66 (v)
risotto, cracked wheat, 112 (v)*
roast chicken with vegetables, 34
rolling out dough, 149
rubbing in butter or margarine, 39

salad,
   summer, 7 (v)
   tomato and mozzarella, 6 (v)
salmon, pan-fried, 22
salt and pepper, adding, 4
sausages,
   cheesy, 122 (v)
   vegetarian, in batter, 134 (v)
scones, 170 (v)
separating eggs, 148
shaping burgers, 11
shortbread, 156 (v)
sifting, 4
simple sponge cakes, 180 (v)
   cherry and coconut, 181 (v)
   chocolate, 181 (v)
   lemon, 181 (v)
slicing,
   peppers 89
   tomatoes, 100
softening onions, 111
soup,
   leek and potato, 8 (v)
   Mexican bean, 110 (v)*
   minestrone, 72
soya bolognese sauce, 114 (v)*
spaghetti
   alla carbonara, 54
   cooking, 53
Spanish omelette, baked, 126 (v)
spiced rice, tropical, 106 (v)*
spinach,
   and ricotta pasta shells, 66 (v)
   cheese flan, 20 (v)

spinach, continued
    strudel, 140 (v)
steak, pan-fried, 22
stir fry,
    vegetable, 26 (v)
    with vermicelli, 74
strawberry trifle, 40 (v)
strudel, spinach, 140 (v)
stuffed,
    pancakes, 16
    peppers, 138 (v)
syrup, measuring, 159

tagliatelle with beef goulash, 32
tart, cheese and tomato, 116 (v)
tasty cookies, 46 (v)
testing a cake, 45, 149
three-bean dip, 102 (v)*
tofu skewers with noodles, 130 (v)
tomato,
    and cheese tart, 116 (v)
    and courgette pizza, 90 (v)
    and mozzarella salad, 6 (v)
    and tuna pasta salad, 76

tomato sauce, 64, 70, 80
    fresh, with pasta, 28 (v)
    with cheese bites, 128 (v)
    with meatballs, 70
    with ravioli, 64
tomatoes, slicing, 100
tortellini, cheesy, 65
tortillas with black bean sauce, 136 (v)
traditional pizza base, 78
trifle, strawberry, 40 (v)
trimming vegetables, 63
tropical spiced rice, 106 (v)*
tuna and tomato pasta salad, 76

vegans, 98
vegetable stir fry, 26 (v)
vegetables, preparing, 98
vegetarian sausages in batter, 134 (v)
veggie burgers, 118 (v)*
vermicelli, with stir fry, 74

weights and measures, 48
whisking egg whites, 173